## "You can do this," she muttered under her breath. "He's just your boss."

*Lies*, her mind whispered. All lies. Not even very good ones. The sad truth was, Sean Ryan was so much more than the man she was currently working for. He was the first man in years who'd been able to…not just sneak past her well-honed defenses, but obliterate them. One smile from him and her knees quivered. One glance from his summer-sky blue eyes and her long-dormant hormones began a dance of joy. Oh, that was humbling to admit, even to herself.

She really didn't need this.

Kate had a good life now. She'd built it carefully, brick by brick, and damned if she'd allow attraction to ruin it all.

Of course, standing strong against what Sean Ryan made her feel would have been much easier if he'd just been able to leave tomorrow as scheduled. But with the blizzard, they could be trapped together for days.

Which brought her right back to the sinking sensation in the pit of her stomach.

# Snowbound with the Boss

# MAUREEN CHILD

First published in Great Britain 2016
By Mills & Boon, an imprint of HarperCollins*Publishers*
1 London Bridge Street, London, SE1 9GF

Large Print edition 2016

© 2016 Maureen Child

ISBN: 978-0-263-06630-2

Our policy is to use papers that are natural, renewable and recyclable products and made from wood grown in sustainable forests. The logging and manufacturing processes conform to the legal environmental regulations of the country of origin.

Printed and bound in Great Britain
by CPI Antony Rowe, Chippenham, Wiltshire

**Maureen Child** writes for the Mills & Boon Desire line and can't imagine a better job.

A seven-time finalist for a prestigious Romance Writers of America RITA® Award, Maureen is an author of more than one hundred romance novels. Her books regularly appear on bestseller lists and have won several awards.

Maureen believes that laughter goes hand in hand with love, so her stories are always filled with humor. The many letters she receives assure her that her readers love to laugh as much as she does. Maureen Child is a native Californian but has recently moved to the mountains of Utah.

To my daughter Sarah—a gift
for which I will always be grateful

# One

Sean Ryan's dreams were of hot beaches, ten-foot waves and ice-cold beer.

His reality was just ice-cold.

January in Wyoming was just…wrong, he told himself. A California guy had no business standing knee-deep in snow. And if he'd had a choice, Sean wouldn't have been there at all.

But it was his turn to change a run-down hotel into a role-playing fantasy based on one of his company's bestselling video games. "Why I couldn't have gotten a damn hotel in Tahiti is a good question, though."

But then, Celtic Knot video games were all based on ancient legends, and as far as Sean knew, there were no legendary Celtic tales set around a beach in Tahiti. Too damn bad.

A tall man, with thick black hair that hung past the collar of the brown leather jacket he wore over sweaters, Sean tucked his hands into the pockets of his jeans and gave a quick look around. The great room of the old hotel was gigantic and echoed with the sound of his footsteps every time his scarred brown boots hit the wooden floor. There were enough windows in the room to make the snow-covered outside feel like the inside. Double-paned glass kept most of the cold out, but even then, so much glass was enough to chill the cavernous room.

The place wasn't huge, only a hundred and fifty rooms, yet it gave the feeling of more. Probably all the wood and glass, Sean told himself. He could see how the hotel would be once the renovations were complete. And God knew there would be plenty of those. Every room needed to be freshened, brought up-to-date and then stocked with gaming systems and flat-screen televisions. They'd get their artists in to do the murals on the walls, bringing the "Forest Run" video game to life and making this a prime destination for gamers from around the country.

And, he had to admit, the setting was perfect to mimic "Forest Run." The hotel sat on two hundred acres of land, with forests, meadows and a wide, beautiful lake. But he couldn't imagine people *wanting* to come to the middle of nowhere in the dead of winter when everything was covered in snow. Who the hell would pick *snow* over *sand*?

Not him, that was for sure. But he had to hope that there were plenty of gamers who actually enjoyed freezing temperatures. As for Sean, he couldn't wait to get back to Southern California. Shaking his head, Sean reminded himself that this trip was almost over. He'd been in Wyoming a week and now that all of the "consultations" with his contractor were finished, he'd be hopping into his company jet that afternoon and getting back to the real world. To his *life*.

Turning his back on the view, Sean glanced toward the ceiling at the sound of footsteps overhead. Instantly, a buzz of awareness shot through him. Scowling, he deliberately pushed aside the feeling, buried it deeply enough that he wouldn't have to acknowledge it.

Nope. When he left, Sean wouldn't miss the cold. Or the solitude, he assured himself. But the woman...that was a different story.

Kate Wells. Businesswoman, contractor, carpenter and current pain in his ass. He was only in Wyoming in the dead of winter because Kate, his contractor on this hotel job, had insisted they needed to meet on-site so she and her crew could get started on the interior renovations.

And from the minute he first saw her, construction work was the last thing on Sean's mind. Instead, he was focused on thick black hair, usually pulled into a ponytail, lake-blue eyes and a mouth wide enough to give a man crazy, sex-fueled dreams.

It had been too long since he'd indulged himself in a really fiery affair, he assured himself.

That's the only explanation for why his body was burning for a woman who wore a damn tool belt, of all things.

He looked toward the ceiling again, the scowl on his face deepening as she moved around upstairs with quick, sure steps. He'd never met a woman as sure of herself as Kate Wells. He'd always admired strong women, but she took things to a whole new level. She argued with him on everything and as irritating as that was, Sean also sort of enjoyed it—which only went to prove that all this cold had frozen and killed off too many of his brain cells.

Shaking his head, he turned on his cell phone and gave silent thanks that at least he had reception out here. Hitting the video-chat button, he dialed and then waited.

On the third ring, his brother Mike's face appeared on the screen.

"I hate Wyoming," Sean blurted.

Mike laughed and leaned back in his desk chair. Right behind his brother, Sean could see the view of the garden behind the old Victorian in Long Beach, California, that served as Celtic Knot's offices. "Don't hold back, tell me how you really feel."

"Funny." Easy for his older brother to be amused, Sean told himself. He wasn't in the middle of a forest with a woman who both attracted and infuriated him. Thinking of Kate, Sean glanced over his shoulder, just to make sure she hadn't sneaked up on him. When he was satisfied, he shifted his gaze back to the phone. Easier to not think of Kate when he was talking about something else entirely.

"It hasn't stopped snowing since I got here," he said. "There's like three feet of snow piling up out there and it's still coming down. I don't think it'll ever stop."

"Sounds cold." Mike gave a dramatic shudder.

"Ha!" Sean snorted. "Beyond cold. Beyond freezing. I'm wearing two sweaters under my jacket—*inside*."

Chuckling, Mike asked, "What's it like when you're not complaining about how cold you are?

Have you managed, in all your misery, to check out the land and the hotel?"

Trust Mike to stay on topic. Sean sighed, then grudgingly admitted, "Yeah, I looked it all over. It's pretty. Lots of trees. Lots of open land. And who knew the sky was so big when you get out of the city?"

"Yeah," Mike said, "I discovered that for myself when Jenny and I were in Laughlin..."

Narrowing his gaze on his brother's image, Sean wondered what the hell had happened exactly between Mike and Jenny Marshall, one of the company's top artists. Mike hadn't talked about it and before Sean had had a decent chance to really interrogate him over it, he'd had to leave for Wyoming.

"Something tells me there's more to that story," Sean mused, promising himself that as soon as he got home again, he'd take Mike out for a few beers and pry the truth out of him.

"If there is," Mike told him, "you're not hearing it."

Not long-distance, anyway. But Sean had never

been one to give up easily. And there was defi-
nitely something going on between his brother
and Jenny. Still, that was for then, and right now
Sean was more interested in getting out of Wyoming before he turned into a Popsicle.

"What's the hotel itself like, Sean?"

"Big. Cold. Empty." Sean blew out a frustrated
breath and pushed one hand through his hair. He
gave another quick look around and gave Mike
a better answer. "The previous owner left some
furniture downstairs, but the bedrooms are a refit
from the ground up. No beds, no chairs, tables,
*nada*."

He shot a glance at the battered leather sofa and
two matching chairs that were drawn up in front
of a massive fireplace in the great room. Sean
didn't think much of the furniture, but since he
and Kate were going to be stuck here for a while,
he was grateful there was more than the floor to
sit on.

"It's no big deal," Mike told him. "We would
have redone the bedrooms the way we wanted
anyway."

"True. And the bones of the place are good." Sean nodded to himself. "A lot of work to do to turn it into a 'Forest Run' fantasy, though."

"And is Kate Wells up to the task?"

"To hear her tell it," Sean muttered. He'd never met a woman so supremely confident in her own abilities. Just as he'd never come up against anyone so willing to argue with him. He was more accustomed to people who worked for him actually *working* for him. But this woman seemed to think *she* was in charge, and that was something he'd have to take care of real damn soon.

"Anyway," he said, once again forcefully pushing Kate out of his mind, "there's a hundred and fifty guest rooms, and they all need work."

Mike frowned. "If we go with your idea to hold our own 'game con' on the property, we'll need more rooms. Are there other hotels close by?"

"No. We're ten miles from the closest. It's a small town with two B and Bs and one motel right off the highway."

Mike's tight scowl deepened. "Sean, we can't go with a big conference if there's nowhere for people to stay." He took a breath and added, "And don't say people can pitch tents."

Sean laughed. "Just because I like camping doesn't mean I want strangers staying all over the property. Anyway, there's a bigger city about twenty-five miles from here, with more hotels." And that was where he was staying. A nice, comfortable, upscale hotel that he would have given anything to be in at that moment. He wanted a shower hot enough to melt the ice chips in his bloodstream. That wasn't going to happen anytime soon, though. "Kate—the contractor had another idea on that problem, too."

"What's she thinking?" Mike picked up his coffee and took a long drink.

Sean glared at his brother as annoyance sharpened his tone. "Is that a cappuccino? You bastard."

Mike grinned and took a longer drink. "I'll enjoy it for you."

"Thanks." The sarcasm was thick, but he knew Mike didn't care. Why the hell would he? Sean wondered. His older brother was at home in Long

Beach with access to their favorite coffee shop, the bar down the street, ocean views and, most importantly, Mike wasn't freezing his ass off.

Damn, Sean missed civilization. Shaking his head, he said, "Kate thinks we should put in some small cabins, behind the main lodge, staggered back into the forest. Give people more privacy, a sense of being out in the wild…"

Mike nodded, thinking about it. "It's a good idea."

"Yeah, I know."

"Yet you don't look happy about it."

"Because she was so damn sure she was right," Sean told him, remembering the conversation from the day before. Kate had had him trudging through snow to inspect the property and the areas she'd already selected for possible cabin sites.

As she'd laid it out for him, he could see it as it would be. Small cabins tucked into the woods would feed in to the fantasy of the place, and he was already considering how they could make each of the cottages different, give them each an identity that would be separate from the rest.

It irritated him, too, that he'd never considered anything like she was suggesting. But damn if the idea hadn't hit home with him. The fact that Kate had come up with it was annoying, but Sean was smart enough to know a good idea when he heard it.

"Yeah," Mike mused. "It's a pain when they're right, isn't it?"

"You have no idea," Sean muttered.

"I think I do." Mike took another deliberate sip of his cappuccino. "Sounds like you're having a great time."

Sean's eyes narrowed into slits. He'd have given his car for a hot cappuccino at that very moment. Just another irritation piled on top of everything else. "Yeah, it's a laugh riot. This woman is the most hardheaded person I've ever dealt with and that includes *you*."

Mike shrugged. "As long as she does good work, that's all you should care about."

His brother was right. That *was* all he should

care about. But it wasn't. Instead, Sean was thinking about her hair, how thick and dark it was, and he couldn't help wondering what it would look like freed from its constant ponytail. He thought about the summer blue of her eyes and the way her tool belt hung low around curvy hips. He hated admitting it even to himself, but whenever she talked, he was so focused on her mouth, he hardly heard what she was saying.

Damn, he had to get out of Wyoming, fast.

Sean scrubbed one hand across his face and focused on the conversation with Mike. "Yeah, yeah. She wants to get her crew in here next week and start in on the rehab, and I don't see a problem with it." He paused and ran one finger around the collar of his black sweater. "As long as I can oversee it from California."

"Okay, but since you didn't take any of the artists with you, what'll she do about the painting we'll need done?"

"Come on," Sean said sharply, "I couldn't bring an artist out here when everyone's doing the final run on 'The Wild Hunt.'"

"True," Mike agreed. "Everyone here's working around the clock."

And Sean should have been. He had to connect with marketing and their clients, check the advertising that was lined up to push the new video game once it was released. Work was piling up for him in California, but he'd had to come out here to get the reno started since he had such a fiery contractor eager for the work to begin. This trip had been bad timing all the way around, really. Every artist at Celtic Knot was focused on the finishing touches of the video game that would be released in the summer, so he hadn't been able to justify pulling them away from their work yet.

"Anyway," Sean continued, "how hard is it to leave walls blank? They can paint it white or something and then when we bring the artists in, they'll have a blank canvas to work on."

"That'll work. You still coming home tomorrow?"

"That's the plan, thank God," Sean said. "Kate's outside, bringing her truck around. We're going to head back to town now. Naturally, it's still snowing."

"If it makes you feel any better, it's seventy-five here today."

"Great. Thanks. That just caps it." A door slammed at the front of the hotel. Kate called out something, and Sean looked to one side and shouted, "What?"

In the next second, Kate was standing in the doorway, shaking her head to send a flurry of fresh snowflakes flying to the floor. "A blizzard's headed in," she said simply.

He covered the phone with his hand. "You're kidding."

"No joke," she said, shrugging. "The pass is already closed. We're not going anywhere."

"For how long?" he demanded.

There was that shrug again. "No way to know."

"Perfect."

"What is it?" Mike asked.

"Karma probably," Sean told him, expressing his disgust. "Kate just heard on the truck radio that the pass down the mountain is closed. I'm snowed in."

Instead of sympathy, Sean watched as Mike unsuccessfully fought back laughter at the situation.

"Thanks for your concern."

Mike held up one hand and tried to stop laughing. "Sorry, sorry."

"How is this funny?" Sean snapped. "I'm trapped in an empty hotel with a crabby contractor and a mountain of snow outside the door."

"Clearly," Mike said finally, "it's only funny from California. But have you got food, heat?"

"We're covered," Kate said, her expression telling him exactly what she thought of the description *crabby*.

"Yeah," Sean said, then he turned to Kate. "Come here for a minute. Meet my brother."

She didn't look happy with the invitation—no surprise there, Sean thought. The woman had a chip on her shoulder the size of a redwood. She walked briskly across the room and stopped beside him to look at the phone screen.

"Hi, I'm Kate and you're Mike," she said, words

tumbling over each other. She spared a quick glance for Sean. "Nice to meet you, but we don't have a lot of time to talk. There's firewood outside, we need to bring it in before the rest of the storm hits. Don't worry, though. There's plenty of food since I make sure my crew is fed while they work and we've been out here this last week taking measurements and getting ideas about the work."

"Okay." Mike threw that word in fast, thinking he probably wouldn't have another chance to speak. He was right.

"The storm'll blow through in a day or two and the plows will have the pass cleared out pretty quickly, so you can have your brother back by the end of the week."

"Okay…"

Sean grabbed the phone and told Kate, "I'll be right there to help. Yeah. Okay." When he looked back at Mike, he was shaking his head. "She's outside bringing in firewood. I've gotta go. And I was this close—" he held up two fingers just a breath apart "—from getting outta Dodge. Now

I don't know when I'll get out. Tell Mom not to worry and don't bother calling me. I'm going to shut off the cell phone, conserve power."

"Okay." In spite of the fact that he'd been amused only a few minutes ago by Sean's situation, now Mike asked, "You sure you'll be all right?"

Sean laughed now. "I'm the outdoors guy, remember? There may not be any waves to surf out here, but I'll be fine. I've been camping in worse situations than I've got here. At least we have a roof and plenty of beds to choose from. I'll call when I can. Just keep a cappuccino hot for me."

"I will. And Sean," Mike added, "don't kill the contractor."

Killing her wasn't what he had in mind, but he wasn't going to admit that to his brother. So instead, Sean said, "I make no promises."

When he hung up and shut off his phone, Sean walked across the room in the direction Kate had disappeared. Damn woman could have waited a minute, he told himself, shaking his head as irritation spiked. He'd already spent a week with her and was walking the ragged edge of control. Now he was going to be snowed in with her for who knew how long.

"This just keeps getting better," he muttered.

He walked through a kitchen that was big enough for their needs but would need some serious renovation. His quick glance covered the amenities he'd already noted earlier in the week. A long, butcher-block island in the middle of the huge room. More of the same counters ringing the perimeter, broken only by an eight-burner stove and a refrigerator that was both gigantic and ancient. The walls were white, yellowed with time and smoke, and the floor was a checkerboard linoleum with chipped-out and missing sections.

The windows were great and normally offered a view of the nearby forest. At the moment, the wide expanse of sky was a dull gray and snow was spitting down thickly enough to resemble a sheet of cotton. The back door was open and led into what Kate had earlier called the mudroom—basically a service porch area with several washers and dryers and a place to stow coats and boots.

Beyond was a covered back porch with a wobbly, needed-to-be-replaced wooden railing. Sean shrugged deeper into his jacket as he stepped into the icy bite of the wind. Snow. Nothing but snow. It was coming down thick and fast and for one split second, Sean could admit to himself that it was pretty. Then he remembered that the "pretty" stuff was currently blocking his only way out, and it quickly lost its appeal.

"Kate?"

"Over here," she shouted.

Zipping his jacket closed, he turned toward her voice and ignored, as well as he could, the cold sharp snap of winter. Snowflakes slapped his face with icy stings and the wind pushed at him as if trying to force him back inside.

He paid no attention to the urge to retreat and instead turned to where Kate was bent over a neatly stacked supply of firewood. She had three split logs in her arms and was reaching for another.

"Let me get it," Sean said, nudging her out of the way.

She whipped her head up to glare at him. "I can handle it."

"Yeah," he said, giving her a nod. He'd seen her stubbornness and her determination to do everything on her own all week. "I know. You're tough. We're all impressed. But if we both get the wood, we can get out of this cold that much sooner."

She looked like she wanted to argue with him, then changed her mind. "Fine. Gather as much as you can, then we'll come back for more."

She headed into the hotel without another word, leaving Sean to grab as many logs as possible. When he straightened, he took another quick look around. Pine trees stood as tall and straight as soldiers on parade, in spite of the heavy, snow-laden wind pushing at them. The lake was frozen over and snowdrifts were piling up at the shore-line. He tipped his head back and stared up at the gray sky as thick flurries raced toward him. The air was thick and cold, and realization settled in on Sean. If this kept up, he could be stuck here for weeks.

* * *

Kate laid the stack of wood in a neat pile beside the stone fireplace, then grabbed the mantel and leaned on it. "The blizzard couldn't have waited to hit until *after* he was gone?"

Of course not. That would have made her life too easy. Way better to strand her here on the mountain with a man who had shaken her nice, comfortable life right down to the ground.

Slowly straightening, she shook her head, hoping to clear out the ragged, disjointed thoughts somersaulting through it. Didn't work, but she pushed through, pushed past. Bending, she took a few of the logs she'd carried in and set them in the hearth. Then she laid down kindling from the nearby basket, took a long wooden match, struck it and held the flame to the kindling until it caught. Taking a minute to get the fire started would help her settle—she hoped.

She watched the fire catch, licking at the wood until the hiss and crackle jumped into the otherwise quiet room.

"You can do this," she muttered under her breath. "He's just your boss."

Lies, her mind whispered. All lies. Not even very good ones. The sad truth was, Sean Ryan was so much more than the man she was currently working for. He was the first man in years who'd been able to not just sneak past her well-honed defenses but obliterate them. One smile from him and her knees quivered. One glance from his lake-blue eyes and her long-dormant hormones began a dance of joy. Oh, that was humbling to admit, even to herself.

She really didn't need this.

Kate had a good life now. She'd built it carefully, brick by brick, and damn if she'd allow attraction to ruin it all.

Of course, standing strong against what Sean Ryan made her feel would have been much easier if he'd just been able to leave tomorrow as scheduled. But with the blizzard, they could be trapped together for days.

And that thought brought her right back to the sinking sensation in the pit of her stomach.

Frowning, she reminded herself that she'd already survived something that would have crushed most people. She could live through a few days in close quarters with Sean.

Nodding in agreement with her silent pep talk, she pushed up from the hearth and turned to get more wood. Sean stalked into the room, arms full of more logs than she could have carried in one trip. He didn't look any happier about their current situation than she did.

Sadly, that didn't make her feel any better.

"Just stack it there on the hearth," she said, waving one hand. "I'll go out for more."

"Yeah," he said, dropping the wood with an ear-shattering clatter. "I'll get the wood. I can carry more than you, so that means fewer trips."

She wanted to argue, but he was right. Still, it was hard for her to accept help. Kate stood on her own two feet. And for the last couple of years especially, she'd deliberately dismissed anyone who thought she couldn't handle things herself.

"Fine," she said. "I've got emergency supplies

out in my truck. I'll get them while you bring in more wood. Get a lot of it. It'll be a long, cold night."

"Right." He paused. "What kind of supplies?"

"Blankets, lanterns, coffeemaker—the essentials."

He gave her a wide smile. "Coffee? Now you're talking. I'd give a hundred bucks for a cup of coffee right now."

Why did he have to smile? Why did that smile have to light up his features, sparkle in his eyes and cause her already-unsteady nerves to wobble and tip dangerously? This whole adventure would be so much easier on her if she could just hate him. Damn it.

"A hundred dollars for coffee?" She nodded. "Sold."

His eyebrows shot up, and that wicked curve of his mouth broadened. "Yeah? Well, I'll have to owe you since I don't have that much cash on me."

Just too much charm, she thought. And he

turned it on and off like a faucet. Her breath caught a little. "That's okay, I'll send you a bill."

"No problem." Amusement drained from his face, but his eyes glittered with promise. "We'll settle things between us before I head back to California. You can count on it."

Oh, boy. Kate watched him go, then turned up the collar of her jacket. She headed for the front door, giving herself a silent, stern lecture as she went. She couldn't believe how that smile of his had affected her. Honestly, he'd been hard enough to resist when he was miserable and complaining about the snow. But a smiling Sean Ryan was even more dangerous.

She stepped outside and welcomed the blast of cold wind and the stinging slap of blowing snow. If anything could put out a fire burning inside, it was a Wyoming winter. But even as she thought it, Kate had to admit that the slow burn of attraction, interest, was still glowing with heat.

She trooped across the wide front porch, down the steps to where she'd left the truck. Snow was already filling up the bed and stacking against the tires. If she left it sitting out here, by the end of the blizzard she and Sean would have to dig out the truck before they could leave. Jumping into the cab, she started it up, then drove around the edge of the old hotel toward the four-car garage standing behind it. She had to jump out of the truck back into the snow to open the door, but once she had her vehicle parked, it was a relief to be out of the wind.

Kate reached over the side of the truck to the metal box in the bed. Unlocking it, she dragged out her stash of emergency supplies. A heavy plastic craft box that she'd commandeered for the purpose, along with a sleeping bag and the two blankets she kept there in case she was ever stranded in the snow.

Heading out of the garage, she closed the door behind her and paused for a moment to look up at the hotel. Sean was no longer on the porch, so he was inside, by the fire. Stranded alone would be a little scary. Stranded with Sean was terrifying.

Oh, not that she was worried about her *safety*. It was more concern for her *sanity* that had her biting her bottom lip as disjointed thoughts bounced off the walls of her mind.

He was too gorgeous. Too smooth. Too rich. And not to mention the fact that he was her *boss*. This one job for Celtic Knot would give her sometimes-floundering construction company a jolt that could keep them going for the next few years.

So it was imperative she keep a grip on the hormones that insisted on stirring whenever Sean was close by. She couldn't afford to give in to what her body was screaming for. An affair with Sean was just too risky. It had been more than two years since she'd been with a man. In that time, Kate had managed to convince herself that whatever sexual needs or desires she'd had, had died with her husband, Sam.

It was lowering to have to acknowledge, even silently, that her theory had been shot to hell by Sean Ryan's appearance in her life.

She shifted her gaze to the hotel, where firelight danced and glowed behind the window glass. Only midafternoon and it was already getting dark.

The wall of snow between her and the hotel was thickening, letting Kate know that this was a big storm. She and Sean could be stuck here for *days*.

How weird was it that she could be both annoyed and excited by the prospect?

# Two

Inside, the fire was already spreading heat around the wide room. Firelight flickered across Sean's features as he bent low to gently lay another log across the already burning wood. He turned his head to look at her, and Kate's breath caught. Fire and light burned in his blue eyes and seemed to settle inside her, where that heat flashed dangerously bright.

A second or two of unspoken tension hummed in the air between them, making each breath she drew a victory of sorts. When she couldn't take it another moment, Kate shattered the spell of silence by speaking. "If you bring in one more load of wood, that should see us through tomorrow."

"Right." He straightened slowly and shoved both hands into the back pockets of his jeans. Nodding at the pile of things at her feet, he said, "You carry a lot of emergency supplies."

Happy to be on safe territory, she glanced down at the things she'd brought inside. "I'd rather be prepared than freeze to death," she told him with a shrug. "You never know when your car won't start or you'll blow a tire or slide on some ice into a ditch..."

"Or get stranded in a blizzard?"

"Exactly." She gave the black nylon sleeping bag a nudge with the toe of her boot, edging it closer to the two wool blankets beside it. "Blankets to keep warm and in the box I've got a battery-operated lantern, PowerBars, chocolate and coffee..."

"There's that magic word again," Sean said with a half grin.

"Finally something we can agree on," Kate answered, a reluctant smile curving her mouth.

Sean's grin only widened, and her heart tripped into a gallop. "Yeah, we've had an interesting week, haven't we?"

"That's one way to put it." Kate sighed, bent down and opened the box to pull out her ancient coffeepot. Snatching the bag of coffee, too, she stood up again and met his steady gaze. "You've argued with every one of my suggestions for this place."

"My place," he said simply. "My decisions."

She'd never had a client fight her on nearly everything before Sean. Normally, Kate didn't mind trying to incorporate a client's wants into the required work. But she also knew what was possible and what wasn't. Sean, though, didn't consider *anything* to be impossible.

"My crew. My work," she countered.

"And here we go again," Sean said, shaking his head. "Yeah, you'll be doing the work, but you're going to do it the way I want it done."

"Even if you're wrong."

His mouth tightened. "If I want it, I'm not wrong."

"You don't know anything about construction," she argued, even knowing it was fruitless. Her hands fisted on the coffeepot and the bag of coffee. The man had a head of solid rock. Hadn't she been hammering at it for the last week?

He pulled his hands from his pockets, crossed his arms over his chest and stood, hipshot, giving her a look of resigned patience. "And how much do you know about video games? Specifically 'Forest Run'?"

"Okay. Not much." This argument was circular. They'd had it several times already, so Kate knew nothing would be settled and still, she had to admit again that he was right.

"Or nothing."

"Fine. Nothing." Her voice sounded defensive even to her, but she couldn't seem to help it. "I'm a little too busy to be wasting my time playing video games."

Briefly, insult flashed across his features.

"Thankfully, there are a few hundred *million* people worldwide who don't feel the same way."

In a heartbeat, he'd reminded her of the difference between them. He was the billionaire. She was the hired help. "You're right," she said, though the words burned her tongue and nearly choked her. "I don't know what gamers would want in a hotel designed especially for them."

He gave her a short, nearly regal nod.

*"But,"* she added, "you don't know about construction. What can and can't be done and more importantly, what should and *shouldn't* be done. You hired me because I'm a professional. When I tell you a wall is load-bearing, it's not because I want to deny you the 'open space to reproduce the sorcerer's meeting rooms.' It's because if I take down that wall it destabilizes the entire building."

His mouth worked as if he wanted to argue, but all he said was, "You have a point."

"Thanks, I thought so."

A brief twist of a smile curved his lips and was

gone again in a flash. "You're the most opinion-ated woman I've ever met."

Kate took a breath. Strange but it was only Sean Ryan who brought out the argumentative side of her. Normally, she found a way to deal with clients with patience and reason. But he pushed every button she had and a few she hadn't even been aware of. She found herself digging in, de-fending her position and never giving ground, which was no way to complete a job. Especially *this* job. She was going to have to learn how to deal with Sean Ryan in a calm, rational way, and she might as well start now. "Okay, I guess you have a point, too."

His eyebrows lifted and amusement shone in his eyes. "Are we having a moment, here?"

Why did he have to be amiable along with ir-ritating? Something inside her flipped over, and Kate took a long, hopefully calming breath. She'd been so solitary, so insulated, since Sam died, being this attracted to a man was staggering. And a little nerve-racking. But all she had to do was get through this storm. Survive being stranded with Sean Ryan long enough to see him get on his private jet and head back to where he belonged. Then everything would get back to normal and she could forget about how he made her feel.

"Why don't you bring more wood and I'll make that coffee."

"And the moment's over," he muttered, shaking his head. "I'll let it go for now, though, since I really want some caffeine."

Kate held her coffeepot and the bag of grounds up like trophies. "The gas is connected. All I have to do is light a pilot light and we can use the stove."

"You're a goddess," he said with a dramatic flair.

Amused, she shook her head. "You're easily impressed."

"Really not," he told her and winked.

He winked, she thought as she walked to the kitchen and got things started. Why did he have to be gorgeous? she wondered. Was it some sort of trick by Fate, to send a man like him to her when she least wanted him?

Mumbling under her breath, she filled a pan with water and used a kitchen match to light one of the gas burners. While she waited for the pot to boil, she headed for the kitchen pantry to look through the food supplies she and her men had left here over the last week.

On normal jobs, they kept a cooler on the job site, stuffed with food, snacks and the guys' lunches. But the hotel job was different. They would be working here for a long time and no doubt with lots of strange hours, so they'd more or less taken over the kitchen to store extra supplies—including paper plates, cups, towels and even, she saw, a plastic bag of disposable silverware.

Smiling to herself, she looked through the snacks and realized she could identify who on her crew had brought them in. Andy had a thing for Cheetos and Paco always had nacho-flavored corn chips with him. Then there were Jack's Oreos and Dave's peanut butter crackers.

Kate herself had brought in chocolate, tea bags and those always-had-to-have Pop-Tarts. Brown sugar and cinnamon, of course.

"Not exactly a five-star restaurant," she murmured a few minutes later, "but we won't starve."

"Yeah?" Sean's voice came from directly behind her, and Kate jumped in response. He ignored her reaction. "What've we got?"

Kate moved away, forcing him to back up, too. "Cheese and crackers. Chips, pretzels and cookies. Everything you probably shouldn't be eating." She glanced at him. "My crew likes their junk food."

"And who can blame them?"

A small smile tugged briefly at her lips. Kate closed the pantry door and opened the refrigerator. "There's more in here, too. The storm hasn't taken out the power yet. That's good. Okay, we've got lots of those little cheese sticks, plus there are three sandwiches from yesterday, too. A few hard-boiled eggs thanks to Tracy, and some macaroni salad."

He frowned. "When we brought lunch for everyone yesterday, there was one sandwich each. I didn't expect leftovers."

"Normally, you'd be right. The crew's usually like locusts, mowing through anything edible— especially if they didn't have to buy it themselves," she said with an affectionate smile for the people she worked with every day. She looked up at him and added, "But thankfully for us, Lilah and Raul are both on diets so they didn't eat theirs and Frank left early because his wife was in labor. So we've got food."

"I forgot about Frank's wife having a baby." Sean leaned against the counter. "What was it, boy or girl?"

"A girl." Kate couldn't stop the smile as she remembered Frank's call late the night before. "He's so excited. They've got four boys already, and he really wanted a girl this time."

"*Five* kids?" Sean asked, then whistled low and long. "Are they nuts?"

He looked so appalled at the very idea, Kate was insulted on behalf of her friends. "No, they're not. They love kids."

"They'd better," Sean muttered and shook all over as if trying to ward off a chill.

"Wow, really hate the thought of family that much?"

Something flickered in his eyes—a shadow— and then it was gone, so fast, Kate wasn't really sure she'd seen it at all.

"No," he said, half turning to lean one hip against the battered kitchen counter. "Just not interested in having one of my own."

"So no driving need to be a father," she said flatly, thinking this was just another insight into the man she would be dealing with for months.

"God, no." He shook his head and laughed shortly. "Can't see me being a father. My brother maybe, but not me."

Though he was brushing it off, Kate remembered that shadow and wondered what had caused it, however briefly. Curiosity piqued, Kate couldn't help asking, "Why?"

He blew out a breath, crossed his arms over his chest and said, "I like having my own space. Doing things on my own time. Having to bend all of that to fit someone else's schedule doesn't appeal to me."

"Sounds selfish," she said.

"Absolutely," he agreed affably. "What about you? If you like kids so much, why don't you have three or four of your own?"

Her features froze briefly. She felt it, couldn't prevent it and could only hope that he didn't notice. One thing she didn't want was to tell Sean about her late husband and the dreams of family they'd had and lost. "Just hasn't worked out that way."

"Hey." Sean moved closer and his voice dropped. "Are you okay?"

"Fine," she said briskly, lifting her chin and giving him what she hoped was a bright—not bitter—smile.

This was simply another reminder of the differences between them, Kate thought. Mister Billionaire Playboy probably thought having a family was like being chained in a cage. But it was all Kate had ever really wanted. She'd come close to having the whole dream—home, husband, kids—but it had been snatched from her grasp and now she was left with only the haunting thoughts of what might have been.

Something Sean clearly wouldn't understand. But that wasn't her problem, was it?

*"Anyway,"* Kate said, "we've got enough food for a few days if we're careful."

"Right." He accepted the change of subject easily enough. "Do we have enough coffee to last?"

*We.* Now they were an unlikely team. As long as the storm lasted, they would be *we.* And she could admit, at least to herself, that in spite of everything, she was grateful not to be stranded up here by herself. Even if it did mean that she and Sean were going to have far too much alone time together.

But for now, dealing with their shared addiction to caffeine took precedence. "I'm on it."

The water in the pan was boiling, so she carefully poured it into the drip filter on her travel pot. She felt Sean watching her. How odd, she thought, that the man's gaze could feel as tangible as a touch. And odder still, she caught herself wishing he *was* touching her, which was just stupid.

For heaven's sake, hadn't she *just* been reminding herself how different the two of them were? How he was temporary in her life—not to mention being her *client*, so in effect, her *boss*. It was undeniable, though. This flash of something hungry between them. It was dangerous. Ridiculous. And oh, so tempting.

It was the situation, she told herself. Just the two of them, stranded in an empty hotel with several feet of snow piling up outside. Of course, her mind was going a little wonky. And the only thing wrong with that explanation was that her mind had been wonky since the moment Sean had arrived in Wyoming.

Over the sound of the howling wind outside, Kate listened to the water plopping through the filter into the coffeepot. A rich, dark scent filled the air, and behind her, Sean inhaled deeply and released the breath on a sigh.

"Man, that smells good."

"Agreed," she said and carefully poured more

water into the filter. While the coffee dripped into the reservoir, Kate walked to the pantry, where she'd stored a few paper supplies for the crew. She grabbed two cups, tossed one to Sean and then turned to the now-ready coffee and poured some for each of them. The first sip seemed to ease some of the jagged edges tearing at her mind.

Leaning back against the counter, she turned to stare out the window above the sink. It was a bay window, with plenty of space for fresh herbs to grow and thrive in the sun. Right now it was empty, but Kate could imagine just how it and everything else about the hotel would look when she and her crew were finished. Still, it was what was happening beyond the glass that had most of her attention.

The snow was coming down so thick and fast, swirling in a wind that rattled the glass panes, she couldn't see past the yard to where the lake stretched out along the foot of the mountains, and the forest was no more than a smudge of darkness in the world of white.

"This happen often?" Sean asked, as he moved up beside her.

His arm brushed against hers, and Kate sucked in a gulp of air to steady herself. "Often enough," she said, determined to get a grip on the rush of something hot and delicious pulsing inside her. Another sip of coffee sent a different kind of heat sweeping through her. "Ask anyone and they'll tell you. If you don't like the weather in Wyoming, wait five minutes. It'll change."

He leaned forward and tipped his head back to see what he could of the sky. "So five minutes from now, the sun should be shining and the snow melted?"

She had to laugh because he sounded so hopeful. "Not likely. This looks like a big one. I figure we're stuck here for a couple of days. Maybe more."

He sighed, nodded and looked at her. "At least we have each other."

And *that*, Kate told herself, was the problem.

They decided to ration what food they had, so an hour later, the two of them split a sandwich and shared a few crackers. Sitting in front of the fire, with the wind and snow pelting the windows, Sean glanced at Kate beside him. They'd pulled the old leather couch closer to the hearth, and now each of them had claimed a corner of the sofa for themselves.

Kate stared into the blaze, and firelight danced across her features and shone in her hair. Her eyes were fixed on the flames, as if looking away from the fire would mean her life. Her behavior told him she was nervous around him. He liked knowing it. Made his own unease a little easier to take.

He frowned to himself as that word reverberated a few times in his mind. *Unease.* Hell, Sean hadn't been uneasy around women since freshman year of high school. Dana Foster—her red hair, green eyes and wide, smiling mouth had turned Sean into a babbling moron. Until he'd kissed her for the first time. That kiss had opened up a world of wonder, beauty and hunger that Sean had enjoyed ever since.

The women in his life—most of them—had

come and gone, barely causing a ripple. Of course, there'd been one woman, years ago, who had affected him, changed him. But he didn't allow himself to think about her or what had happened between them. Ancient history that had nothing to do with who and what he was today.

Now there was Kate. And what she did to him was so much more than that long-ago woman. Admitting that really bothered him and acted as a warning bell. Kate had him tied into knots, and he didn't appreciate it. She made him feel nearly desperate to have her. And while his body clamored for him to go for it, those warning signals continued to ring out in his brain, telling him to keep his distance and to get the hell away from her as fast as he could. But that wasn't going to happen, thanks to this blizzard.

He'd avoided any kind of entanglements for years and wasn't looking for one now. But logic didn't have a lot to do with anything he was feeling at the moment.

He wanted her. Wanted her badly enough that his mind was filled with images of her all the damn time. When he was with her, his body was tight and hard, and the longer he was with Kate, the worse it got. That need clawed at his insides, demanding release. Still, sex with her would only complicate matters, and Sean was a man who didn't like complications.

His life would have been a lot easier if only he'd been able to escape Wyoming and put several hundred miles between himself and Kate. That wasn't going to happen, though, so he had to find a way to survive this enforced closeness.

"Why are you staring at me?"

He came out of his thoughts and focused on the woman now looking at him. "Just thinking."

"Now I'm worried," she said, a half smile curving her mouth. "Thinking about what?"

Well, he wasn't going to tell her the truth—that he was thinking about how soon he could get her out of her clothes—so he blurted out something that had been on his mind lately. "Wondering how you became a contractor."

Her brow furrowed, her eyes narrowed and he had the distinct feeling she didn't believe him. But then she shrugged and answered.

"My dad is the easy answer," she said, shifting her gaze back to the fire snapping and crackling just a few feet away from them. "He's a master carpenter. Started his own business when I was a kid." She smiled in memory, and Sean noticed how her features softened. "I used to work for him every summer and he and the guys on his crew taught me everything I know about construction."

"Funny, I worked summers for my dad, too," Sean said, remembering how he had tried desperately to get out of work so he could go surfing instead.

"What's your dad do?"

"Lawyer," Sean said, bracing his hands on the floor behind him. "He wanted my brother and I to go to law school, join his firm."

"No interest in being a lawyer?" she asked.

He shuddered. "No. When you worked for your dad, you were outside, right?"

"Usually, yeah."

"Not me. Dad had us shredding old documents, sweeping, mopping and in general doing everything the building custodians needed us to do."

He shook his head. "Hated being locked up inside, so I promised myself that I'd find a job where I could take off and go surfing when I wanted to."

She laughed. "Not many employers allow surfing breaks, I imagine."

"Nope." He grinned and added, "Just another reason I like being my own boss. You'd know what I mean by that."

She nodded. "Yeah. I do."

A moment or two of silence, broken only by the snap and hiss of the fire, stretched out between them. It was almost companionable, Sean thought. It was the first time since he'd met Kate Wells that they'd gone so long without an argument. It surprised him how much he was enjoying it.

"So," he asked, "who'll run things for you while you're stuck here?"

"With a blizzard this heavy, the guys will just hole up at their homes and take a few days off. They won't be expecting to work through it," she said, then looked around the room.

It was filled with shadows that moved and shifted in the flickering light. "As soon as the snow stops and the roads are clear, we'll get started on the renovations. The structure's sound, but for needing some new shingles on the roof and some of the porch railings replaced. We'll be working on the inside for now, of course, and move to the outside when spring finally gets here—"

"And we're talking about work again," Sean interrupted her. He'd noticed that whenever their conversations threatened to get personal, she "ran home to mama" so to speak and turned to talk of the job.

"Your fault this time. Besides, work is why we're here," she pointed out.

"No," he argued with a wave of his hand toward the closest window that displayed a view of swirling white, "snow is why we're here. We've talked about the job enough for today."

"Well then," she said abruptly, "what do you want to talk about?"

"Who says I want to talk at all?" he asked and gave her a slow smile.

She stiffened and her features went cool and dispassionate. What did it say about him, Sean wondered, that her reaction only fed the hunger gnawing at him? This woman's obvious reluctance to admit to what was simmering between them only intrigued him further.

So maybe, he told himself, the secret to surviving close quarters with Kate was to go ahead and give in to the sexual tug happening. If they tried to ignore it, the next few days were going to be misery.

"Yeah," she said, "that's not going to happen."

"Never say never," he told her with a careless shrug. "We're stuck together and I'm pretty damn charming."

A hesitant smile twitched at her lips briefly. "I think I can control myself."

"We'll see, won't we?" He was a man who loved a challenge. And Kate Wells was surely that.

"Right. I think I'll bring in more wood." She pushed herself to her feet and looked down at him.

"Thought we had enough." He glanced at the

high stack of split logs he'd already carried in and set beside the hearth.

"Can't have too much," she said, pulling her jacket on.

He knew a displacement activity when he saw one. She was trying to get some space, some distance from him, and damn if he was going to let her. "I'll get it."

"I can do it," she said and left without another look at him.

Muttering under his breath about hardheaded women, Sean grabbed his jacket and followed. He walked through the mudroom and stepped out onto the wide, covered back porch in time to see Kate grabbing several big logs. "Let me get it."

"I said I don't need help," she countered.

Sean came up beside her just as she whirled around to face him. Her elbow caught him in the chest, and he took a step back and hit the edge of the top step. Off balance, his arms windmilled as he felt himself falling and knew he couldn't stop it. The fresh snow cushioned his fall and puffed up around him in a cloud. He was flat on his back, staring up at still more snow falling out of a steel-gray sky.

"Oh, God, are you okay?" Kate dropped the wood she held and reached out one hand to him. "I didn't know you were there, really."

Sean only stared at her. Snowflakes gathered in her hair, on her lashes, on the collar of her coat. Her hand was out toward him, and he grabbed it. But rather than take her help to get out of the snow, he gave a hard yank and pulled her down to join him.

She gave a half shriek when she landed on top of him, then immediately struggled to push herself up again. But having her body pressed along his felt so good, Sean was in no hurry to release her.

"What's the rush?" he asked, mouth just a breath away from hers.

"It's freezing."

"Cuddle up, we'll keep each other warm."

# Three

"You're crazy," she said with a shake of her head. Thick, heavy snowflakes kept falling all around them, landing on his lashes, his cheeks.

"And charming. Don't forget charming."

"Right," she said, laughing. Damn it, he really was charming. Most men getting pushed into a snowdrift wouldn't have been so nice about it—though he'd made sure to yank her into the wet cold just to keep things even. "Pulling me into the snow? Charming."

He grinned. "You started it."

She had. And now that she was lying on top of

him, she couldn't really regret it. "You're enjoying this, aren't you?"

He slid one hand down her spine toward her behind, and her eyes flashed in warning. "Yeah. I guess I am."

"Like I said. Crazy."

"Kiss me once and we'll get out of this snow."

Kissing Sean Ryan was absolutely not a good idea. But oh, she was tempted. Tempted enough that she knew she'd give in if she didn't move.

"I'm going in now," she told him and pushed against him again, trying to lever herself up.

Sean held on to her. "One kiss. See if we can melt all this snow."

Her gaze dropped to his mouth then lifted to meet his eyes. Temptation had never looked so good, she thought, knowing that she was in far deeper water than she'd ever been in before. No, she wasn't some shy virgin. She was a widow. And the man she had loved and married had been *nothing* like Sean.

Sam Wells had been sweet, kind, soft-spoken. An easygoing man with a ready smile and a gentle nature. Kate wasn't used to dealing with a man who wore arrogance and confidence like a second skin. And blast it, she couldn't understand why she found him so…attractive.

Then, while her thoughts were muddled and her defenses down, Sean tugged her closer and closed his mouth over hers.

So much heat. It was a wonder the snow they were lying in didn't melt into slush.

While her body lit up like a glowing neon sign, Kate's mind flashed a warning. *Melt snow?* If he kept this up, Sean would melt her *bones*.

Pull away, she told herself. Stop this now. But she wasn't going to stop and she knew it. It had been so long—*too* long—since she'd been held, kissed. That was why she was reacting so wildly to Sean's touch, she assured herself. It wasn't personal. It was simply a biological need that hadn't been so much as acknowledged for two years.

But when his tongue tangled with hers, she had to admit, at least silently, that it was this man causing her reaction. Not just a kiss, but Sean's kiss.

For a week, she'd worked with him, argued with him and, yes, dreamed about him. Now his hands were on her, his mouth was devouring hers and all she could think was *more*. This was so unlike her. So out of the realm of her ordinary world she had no idea what to do or how to handle it.

He broke the kiss, stared at her as if she'd just dropped out of the sky from Mars, then shook his head. "Well, damn. If I'd known what kissing you would be like, I'd have done it a week ago."

Gazing into his beautiful blue eyes, she blurted out before she could stop herself, "I might have let you."

One corner of his truly fabulous mouth tipped up. "Might?"

He already thought far too much of himself, so no way was she going to feed an ego that was already strong enough for three healthy men.

"I think we're way past 'might,' Kate," he said, his fingers rubbing at the base of her neck until she wanted to purr in reaction.

That realization made Kate pull back, shake her head. "No, we are not going to do this."

"Not here, anyway," Sean agreed. "We'll freeze to death."

Not the way she was feeling at the moment, Kate thought. Despite the cold, the snow, the icy chill of the wind, she felt only the heat. That was the problem. Determined to put some space between them, Kate shoved herself to her feet. Sean did the same, then caught her elbow in a firm grip.

"You're going to pretend nothing happened?"

"It was a kiss, Sean. That's all." She slipped out of his grasp, pulled off her cap, tore the band from her hair and shook it free until it lay thick around her shoulders.

"A hell of a kiss, Kate."

She felt the imprint of his fingers right through her jacket and sweater as if he was touching her bare skin. What would it be like if he *actually* touched her? Oh, don't think about that…

"Kate—"

"We need to get more wood."

"Oh, I've got plenty of wood."

He gave her a slow smile as his eyebrows arched. Kate blew out a breath. Well, she'd walked right into *that* double entendre. "Funny."

He grinned. "Told you I'm charming."

"You shouldn't waste it on me," Kate told him.

"Who says it's a waste?"

Kate sighed, tipped her head to one side and stared at him. "Why are you doing this?"

"We're *both* doing this, Kate," he said flatly. Moving in, he closed what little distance lay between them. His hands came down on her shoulders and though she knew she should shrug him off, she didn't. That stirring of bone-deep heat was too irresistible. Too compelling.

In this world of swirling white and icy cold, it was as if they were the only two people alive. As if nothing beyond this old hotel existed. Mattered. She stared up at him, into those blue eyes, and felt herself weakening further.

He was so damn sure of himself, Kate thought. And as her willpower dissolved like sugar in hot water, she told herself he had every right to be.

She'd had no intention of giving in to this attraction between them, and now she couldn't think of anything else.

"So, what's it going to be?" He looked down into her eyes as he slid his hands up from her shoulders to cup her face. The chill of his hands on her skin skittered through her and was swallowed by the building fire inside. "Are we gonna spend the next few days pretending nothing's happening between us?"

"It's the safest thing to do."

"You always take the safe route?" His mouth curved.

Yes. She'd lived most of her life trying to be safe. Her mother had died in a car accident when Kate was a girl, and that incident had marked her. She always buckled her seat belt. Drove the speed limit. Safety—caution in all things, was paramount. In everything from driving to balancing her checkbook to salting her steps during winter. She didn't take chances. Risks. She was always careful. Always vigilant. And the smart thing to do right now would be to continue being safe. To walk away from what she felt when she was with Sean.

Even while she was giving herself some excellent advice, he bent his head and kissed her. Once. Twice. His mouth was soft, his manner tender and she was lost. When he finished, leaving her breathless and just a little unsteady, he looked at her again.

Kate swallowed hard and said, "Safe is smart."

"Be stupid," he urged.

She couldn't look away from that warm, determined gaze. "I think I'm going to."

He kissed her again. This time gentle tenderness washed away in a roaring tide of clawing, greedy hunger that had been building between them for days. Even through the thick layer of sweaters and jackets they wore, Kate felt his hard, muscled chest pressed against her, and everything inside her caught fire.

It was as if embers that had lain smoldering within suddenly caught a draft of air that flashed them into flames. Her hands at his shoulders, she clung to him as he wrapped his arms around her waist and held her tight, close. Though they stood locked together in knee-deep snow, she didn't feel the cold. His mouth fused to hers, his breath filled her, his tongue twisted with hers and Kate felt the already-blazing fire inside her erupt and flash white-hot.

He tore his mouth from hers and said, "Inside. We'll freeze to death out here."

"So not cold," she told him, licking her lips to savor the taste of him.

He grinned, and her heart stumbled. "Gonna make sure you stay that way, too."

Keeping one arm locked around her, he guided her into the hotel, through the kitchen door, then slammed it closed behind them. They left the wind, the snow, the cold, and now it was just the two of them.

Nerves rose up unexpectedly and Kate started thinking. Her body was churning, every hormone she possessed was doing a cha-cha of anticipation, but her brain had clicked back on the moment he stopped kissing her and now...

"No way," he said, caging her against the counter, with his hands braced on either side of her.

"What?" She blinked up at him.

"You're thinking too much. You're starting to worry that maybe we're making a mistake."

"Are you a mind reader now?" she asked, trying to ignore the hard thump of her heartbeat.

He laughed shortly. "Reading your mind isn't that tough at the moment." His gaze moved over her face like a caress before meeting her eyes again. "You're interested. You just don't want to be."

"I could say the same about you," she pointed out in her own defense.

"Yeah, you could." He nodded thoughtfully. "The difference between us is I'm not big on denying myself and you seem to be a champ at it."

"I'll agree with the first half of that sentence. You do seem to be the type who indulges himself whenever he feels like it."

"Why not?" he asked with a shrug. "You don't get trophies from the universe for being stoic and cheating yourself out of something that could be amazing."

In spite of everything, Kate felt a rush of anticipation that fed a small smile. The man was arrogance personified. "You're so sure it would be amazing?"

His mouth curved, his eyes gleamed and he leaned in closer until their mouths were just a breath apart. "Aren't you?"

Stray snowflakes slipped from the collar of her jacket, went beneath the neckline of her sweater and snaked along her spine. Kate shivered and told herself it was the ice on her skin, not the heat in his eyes that had caused it.

"This is crazy," she murmured, shifting her gaze from his eyes to his mouth and back again.

"I'm a big fan of crazy," he whispered.

"Yeah, you would be," Kate said with a choked-off laugh.

Her insides jumped, trembled and settled into a thrum of expectancy that wouldn't be denied. Crazy is just what they were talking about here. Sex with Sean would be a mistake. A huge one.

But if she let this moment pass, let him go back to California without taking the opportunity Fate had handed her, wouldn't that be a mistake, too? Wouldn't she have to live with regret for the rest of her life?

And she couldn't handle more regrets.

Kate had been so closed off for the last two years, she'd never once felt even the slightest attraction for a man. And what she felt for Sean went light-years beyond a "slight attraction." That could be a problem, too, she knew. Feeling too much was an open invitation to pain.

Kate had already had enough pain to last a lifetime.

So she'd have to keep her heart tucked neatly away. Of course, sex without love wasn't like her at all. But then again, she'd already had and lost love and didn't expect to ever have it again. So unless she wanted to live her entire life as if she was locked up in a monastery, she'd have to accept that things, for her, had changed. Affection would have to be enough. And as she met his eyes, Kate could admit to herself that as much as Sean irritated and annoyed her, she also sort of liked him. Hard not to, really. Looking up into Sean's eyes, Kate thought he really was as charming as he claimed to be. Plus he didn't cheap out on building plans, he was fair to her crew and even when he argued with her, he managed to make her laugh.

That kind of man was hard to resist. Though she'd been doing her best to do just that for the last week, she was done with it now. She took a breath and sighed heavily. She was finished trying to ignore the buzz of electricity between them.

If she was going to make a mistake, Kate preferred it be an active decision, not a mistake of omission.

"So, Kate," he murmured, pushing the edge of her jacket aside to drag the tips of his fingers along the undersides of her breasts. "Are we going to be crazy together, or are we going to be sad and lonely separately?"

She shivered again as tiny twists of heat licked at her. Her eyes closed briefly and when she opened them again, Sean was there, staring into her gaze, searching for her answer.

She lifted one hand, cupped his face and drew him to her. "Crazy," she whispered. "I vote for crazy."

"Thank God." He kissed her.

Kate's entire body lit up in an explosion of light and color and heat. She hooked her arms around his neck and hung on, drawing him even closer. Now that she'd opened the floodgates of long-banked desires and needs, she was helpless to do anything but ride the tide cresting inside her. Kate groaned as he parted her lips with his tongue. That fast, greedy dance stole her breath, blurred her mind and set fire to her body.

His hands were busy, too, pushing her jacket off her shoulders and down her arms. Free, Kate did the same for him, then threaded her arms back around his neck as he lifted her and plopped her down onto the old, worn counter. He moved to stand between her thighs, and she hooked her legs around his waist.

They were eye to eye now and when he scraped his hands up beneath the hem of her sweater to cup her breasts, even through the fragile material of her bra, Kate felt heat blossom. Tingles flickered into life deep in her belly, and the core of her ached and throbbed in time with the beat of her heart.

*Want*. Desperate, frantic need clawed at her, and Kate threw herself into the conflagration. Outside, snow flew in an icy wind that rattled the windowpanes and slammed a stray shutter against the side of the hotel. Neither of them noticed or cared.

"Other room," Sean muttered thickly, tearing his mouth from hers. "By the fire."

"Not cold," she assured him, leaning in for another kiss.

He indulged her, once, twice, then pulled back and shook his head. "Nope. Want you naked and," he added, "in this room, we'll both be too cold to finish what we started."

He was right. The kitchen was cold and getting colder. The light was going outside, and the snow piling up was seeping its icy touch through the walls. True, the heat inside her was only building, but the thought of being with him in front of a roaring fire had its appeal.

"Right," she said, giving him a nod, "let's go."

He scooped her off the counter and braced his hands on her behind. Kate kept her legs wrapped around his hips and held on while he carried her to the great room. At any other time, she might have objected to being toted around, but she was too busy enjoying the feel of his hard body pressed against her center. She went hot and wet, her own body trembling in wild anticipation. She wriggled against him, and he sucked in a gulp of air.

"Keep moving like that and we'll never make it to the fire."

"There's plenty of fire here already," she told him.

He glanced at her, his features tight, his eyes flashing with purpose, then quickened his steps. Kate grinned because she felt the same way. *Hurry, hurry.*

Now that she'd made the decision to be with him, she didn't want to wait another second. She wanted him on her, inside her. She wanted him to claim what she'd only given to one other man before him.

A brief flicker of guilt sprang up in the recesses of her mind, but she smothered it. There was no room for thoughts of anyone else, of other times, other lives and loves. For this moment, there was only her…and Sean.

Sex. She hadn't been with a man in more than two years. That had to be the reason she was reacting so wildly to Sean's caresses. Always before, the best part of sex for Kate was the closeness, the snuggling that came after. She'd never before known this kind of hunger—hadn't really believed she was capable of it. Now, Kate had to fight her sense of guilt for admitting even to herself that Sean was making her feel more than her husband ever had—but that was for later. For now, all she wanted was an end to the driving demands within.

And that's when it hit her. They couldn't do this. "No. No, wait."

"Oh, no," Sean said with a dramatic moan. "Please don't tell me you're changing your mind."

"No, it's not that," she said, licking her lips, swallowing the knot of disappointment that seemed to be lodged in her throat. "I'm not on the pill, and we don't have protection—"

In the great room, he made straight for the rug in front of the hearth. He set her on her feet, grinned down at her and reached into his back pocket for his wallet, then pulled out what looked like an entire string of gold-foiled condoms.

Her eyes widened, then she smiled and shook her head. "Are you a teenager? You carry condoms in your wallet?"

"Since I met you—" he grinned "—yeah. You bet." He handed the condoms to her, then reached down for the sleeping bag she'd carried in earlier. "You have your emergency supplies...I have mine."

Kate didn't know whether to be flattered or worried. He'd planned this. Came prepared to have sex with her several times—judging by just how many condoms he'd tucked into his wallet. Her stomach jittered with nerves. She'd only ever been with one man. Her late husband, Sam. She remembered being stirred by his kisses, his caresses. She remembered the climbing tension inside her, and she remembered the soft *pop* of release that was both fulfilling and somehow disappointing.

And now, she was willingly racing down that same road with a man she barely knew. She must be crazy, Kate decided. It was the only explanation.

Sean snatched up the sleeping bag she'd carried inside earlier. Untying it, he flipped it out onto the rug, then bent to unzip it and open it to its full width.

"Not a king-size bed at the Ritz," he told her, "but it'll do."

There were those nerves again, skittering wildly in the pit of her stomach. Firelight danced and shifted across the sleeping bag and sent twisting, writhing shadows around the empty room. She watched him, caught by his steady, direct gaze, and felt the last of her doubts, her hesitation, slide away. Kate had made her decision and she wouldn't second-guess herself now. Sean was right in that they'd come too far to stop—

and more importantly, Kate didn't *want* to stop. "Works for me."

She put all thought aside and eagerly went into his arms when he reached for her. With the fire crackling and sizzling behind them and warmth slowly filling the massive room, they frantically pulled at each other's clothing. A wild, clamoring rush of need nearly choked her, and Kate couldn't even imagine why she'd been so nervous only moments before.

Sweaters were tossed to the floor, her bra was tugged free and dropped. His hands covered her breasts, his thumbs and fingers pulling and tweaking at her already-rigid nipples until Kate groaned and arched into his touch, silently demanding more. She didn't think. Couldn't have, even if she'd wanted to. There was only feeling now. Deep wells of sensation opening up inside her, spilling through her bloodstream like liquid gold.

Nothing in her memories of times with Sam could have prepared her for what Sean was doing to her. She'd never been this electrified before.

Never known the sizzle of her own flesh or the burn at her center.

"You feel even better than I thought you would," he whispered, magic fingers still showering gentle torture on her breasts.

"Oh, I feel *great*," she agreed and leaned into him, sliding her hands up under the hem of the black T-shirt he'd worn beneath his sweater. His body was sharply defined muscles and warm, soft skin. She pulled at the shirt in frustration until he let her go long enough to yank it off himself. Then he drew her close, holding her against him tightly, skin to skin, body to body.

She wouldn't have thought there was more to feel, more to *want*, but there was. Sean showed her just how much. Kate had never felt like this before. Hadn't known she *could*. Her brain was muddied, her breath coming in short, hard gasps. A tingling sensation crept through her veins, making her body feel alight. Tension tightened inside her, and she yearned for that soft, delicious shimmer of release she knew was waiting for her. It would ease the unbearable pressure building within and take the edge off the desire pumping through her. She didn't want to wait another minute.

Tugging at him, she pulled Sean down to the sleeping bag with her. And the icy feel of the black nylon against her heated flesh was a counterpoint to what he was doing to her, adding yet another layer of sensation to the feelings driving her wild.

He leaned over her, stared down into her eyes and Kate's system jolted into overdrive. The man had a great face. And an amazing mouth that he fused to hers in the next instant. A muffled groan tore from her throat as she met every twist of his tongue against hers. She took his breath and gave him hers. Her hands scraped up and down his bare back, loving the smooth glide of hot flesh beneath her palms.

The fire snapped, hissed. The snow pelted the windows and the wind moaned beneath the eaves. And all of it was background music to what was happening between them. Here, in this room, there was no place for cold or ice. There was only the building heat.

He cupped her core and even through her jeans, her body responded with a jolt. Her hips lifted, rocked into his touch as she pulled free of his kiss and gasped for the air her screaming lungs demanded. This was so much more than she'd expected. That tiny shimmer of release she was hoping for couldn't come soon enough.

"You're amazing," he whispered, dipping his head to kiss the side of her throat, to drag the tip of his tongue up and down the pulse point pounding with her response to his touch.

She could hardly hear him over the hammering beat of her own heart. It was thunder in her ears, muffling the world around her. But she didn't care. All she cared about was this man's hands on her and the pleasure she knew was waiting for her. When he unzipped her jeans and swiftly tugged them down her legs and off, she was frantic.

All that stood between her and his touch were the black lace panties she wore. Helpless to do anything else, Kate lifted her hips again in invitation, in silent plea. Her body was buzzing, throbbing with a desperate need that only he could meet.

"Well, now," Sean said, smiling, "if I'd known you had something like that hidden underneath those jeans, we might have gotten to this point sooner."

She took a breath, shuddered. "I've got a weakness for lingerie."

"And I'm pleased to know it," Sean said, eyes gleaming. "Though at the moment, we really don't need these, do we?"

She shook her head as he hooked his fingers beneath the fragile elastic band and slid the swatch of black lace down her legs. Then he sat back and looked her over, up and down. His gaze was as thorough as a touch and just as sensual. Kate moved beneath his steady regard, loving the flash in his eyes as he watched her.

She reached up for him, but Sean pulled back then stood and quickly tore off the rest of his clothes. He grabbed his emergency supply of condoms, tore one off and in seconds, sheathed himself and turned back to her. He slid his body along hers until Kate wanted to whimper with the sheer beauty of it. He was hard and strong, and she wanted him more than ever.

Reaching one hand down, she wrapped her fingers around his hard length and smiled at his hiss of an indrawn breath. She stroked him, watched his blue eyes darken and gleam in reaction and knew that he was as desperate as she to end this torment.

"That's it," he muttered thickly and moved to kneel between her thighs.

"Yes," she whispered, reaching for him again. "Please. Now."

"Oh, yeah," he vowed. "Now."

In one long thrust, he entered her and Kate's body splintered. The soft release she'd been expecting rolled through her, and she relaxed a little, knowing that the hum her body still felt was just what was expected of being so twisted up into desire. She was accustomed to this, too. The vague sense of disappointment that kept her body buzzing expectantly in spite of what she'd just experienced. In an hour or two it would fade and she wouldn't feel the frustration anymore.

Lifting one hand to his face, she smiled up at him. "Thanks."

His mouth quirked, and he held perfectly still, his body locked with hers. "You're thanking me?"

"Well...yeah."

That smile of his broadened into a grin. "Save your thanks for when we're finished."

Well, sure, she thought. He wasn't finished. He would be soon, though, and then she could lie against him for a while, feel that warmth of the afterglow that had always been the best part of sex for her.

"Right," she said and lifted her hips as he began to move inside her. Again and again, his body claimed hers until the tension in Kate's body ratcheted up even higher than it had been before. She gasped, shook her head from side to side and clung to his arms, his shoulders. This had never happened before. Not for her. Always with Sam, there was that small release, then his body collapsing on top of hers and then the quiet while her racing heart tried to calm.

There was no calm here. Only the frantic need

pulsing inside her like a neon sign. Sean slid one hand down the length of her, to where their bodies joined and he touched her. Kate's eyes flew open as he caressed that single, sensitive spot at the very center of her. Surprise, shock and a wild, raw pleasure rocked her to her bones. She shrieked his name as her body bucked beneath his. A wave of incredible, explosive sensations shattered her, and all she could do was hold on and fight to survive the ride.

"That's it," Sean whispered, leaning down to kiss her, hard. "Now go again."

"No," she gasped. Unthinkable. She couldn't take any more. "Impossible. Can't. Catch. My. Breath."

She hadn't known her body could do something like that. Feel so much. Take so much. And yet, even while she told Sean she couldn't do it again, that down-low tingle churned into life at her core. She'd never live through this, she told herself, and then a quiet, satisfied voice in her brain whispered, *Who cares?*

A heartbeat later, thought ended and her body

picked up where her mind left off. She and Sean came together frantically, each of them racing to give. To take. To feel. Seconds spun into minutes and the two of them rolled across that sleeping bag as if it was a luxurious bed.

Breathing labored, hearts pounding in tandem, they moved as one, two more shadows in the flickering light. When the next shattering orgasm slammed into her, Kate dragged his mouth down to hers and swallowed his shout, as this time their bodies erupted together…and holding each other, they tumbled over the edge of the abyss.

Later, he scraped his palms along her back and down to the curve of her behind. Kate trembled at his touch, at the still-so-fresh memory of what he could make her feel. "I'm not done with you yet," he said, his voice barely more than a low growl of promises and demands.

"Good," she said, rolling to one side and dragging him over on top of her again. "I'm not done with you, either."

He grinned. "My kind of woman."

For now, anyway, she told herself.

# Four

The fire was dying, there was a warm, lush, naked woman asleep in his arms and Sean couldn't relax. Hell, he should be in a relaxation *coma* after everything the two of them had shared over the last few hours. Instead, he was wide-awake, staring into the fire, *thinking*.

So far, he didn't much care for his thoughts, either. Scrubbing one hand across his face, he tightened the hold he had on Kate when she curled into him and nestled her head on his chest. Her hair was soft and thick and smelled like strawberries. Her breath drifted across his skin and when she sighed, the small sound seemed to ripple through him.

It had been years since he'd actually slept with a woman he'd slept with—which hardly made sense and almost made him smile—until he remembered the only other woman he'd held like this in the night. Then all thoughts of smiles faded away and shadows fell across his mind. This wasn't the same thing at all, he assured himself. Kate wasn't Adrianna, and the situation was completely different.

God. Adrianna. He hadn't allowed himself to so much as think her name in years. He'd deliberately wiped her face from his memories, closing the door firmly on a past that might have haunted him otherwise.

So he wouldn't dredge up all of that now, either. This was Kate and though he didn't like admitting it, sex with her had been…*more* than he'd ever experienced before. With anyone. But that didn't necessarily mean a damn thing. Sure, Kate's responses had driven him beyond simple pleasure into a realm he'd never thought to enter—but that didn't mean he wanted to stay there.

His body stirred when Kate sighed again in her sleep and slid one arm across his chest. All right. Maybe he *did* want to stay there. At least temporarily. Sean looked down at her and admired the flicker of light and shadow that danced over her skin. Beautiful and strong and confident. She intrigued him. Worried him. Okay, he admitted, *fascinated* him. Acknowledging as much, even to himself, bothered the hell out of him.

His body had been at a slow burn since the moment he'd met Kate. But sex was supposed to have taken care of that. Eased the itch. It hadn't come close. Instead, he only wanted her again. And feeling like that wasn't in the game plan.

Frowning, Sean dragged the edge of the sleeping blanket over the two of them, as the fire died and a chill snaked through the big room. He should get up to stoke the flames, but moving would wake her up and...hell, he thought. Why bother lying to himself? He didn't want to get up because it felt too good lying there with her sprawled across him.

Outside, the wind was still shrieking, snow still pelting the window glass. Without that fire, it'd get damn uncomfortable in there. He'd have to let go of Kate soon and rebuild the fire before they froze to death. But he wasn't ready to do that just yet, and that realization bothered him, too.

This whole situation had *mess* written all over it. He'd come here to work and landed himself trapped in a snowbound hotel with the one woman who could get to him faster than anyone else had in years. He had to pull back for both of their sakes. Neither of them was interested in a damn relationship. He had to remember that as good as this was between them, it wasn't going anywhere. He wouldn't *allow* it. But that didn't mean he wouldn't enjoy this time with Kate for as long as it lasted.

"I feel…amazing," she whispered, her soft voice breaking into his thoughts. Sean was grateful.

He looked down at her and met her gaze as she

lay watching him. She really did feel amazing, he told himself, and that was part of the problem. But right now, he didn't give a good damn.

He looked into her eyes, smoothed her hair back from her face. She'd slept for an hour or so. Long enough. "You know I'm still not done, right?"

A slow, incredibly sexy smile curved her mouth. "I'm really glad to hear that."

Sean took hold of her and pulled her up until their mouths met, until she sighed and he tasted her, swallowing her breath, making it a part of him. Then he rolled them over, levering himself over her, taking all she had to give. He lost himself in her, let the rest of the world outside that room slide away and closed his mind to thoughts of anything but this moment.

Tomorrow could take care of itself.

The next morning, Kate felt well used and limber. Her body ached in a good way and though she should have been exhausted, instead she felt energized—as if she could grab her tools and renovate the entire hotel by herself. She'd had no idea she could feel this good.

Smiling to herself, Kate made coffee and stared out the window at the world of white. The snow was still coming down and the straight-as-a-soldier pines were beginning to bow beneath the weight of the heavy, wet snow on their branches. This was a big storm showing no signs of ending yet—and she was glad. In fact, she'd never been so happy about being snowed in.

Logically, of course, Kate knew this wasn't the most brilliant move she'd ever made. Getting involved sexually with her boss was crazy, but at the moment, she really couldn't regret it. That, she knew, would come later. But for now, all she could do was marvel at the memories of everything Sean had done with her—and to her.

A flush of heat rushed through Kate, tingling across her nerve endings until she felt as if her skin was burning. Until she put a stop to it. Last night, she'd been so swept away by what she was feeling, there hadn't been time for guilt to grab hold of her. Now, there was too much time.

Everything she'd experienced with Sean was fresh in her mind, and Kate couldn't help feeling disloyal to the husband she had lost. As much as she had loved her husband, Kate was forced to acknowledge that Sam had never made her feel what Sean had. During her marriage, Kate had assumed that it was her own fault that somehow, something was lacking that kept her from experiencing the mind-shattering orgasms her friend Molly loved to describe in intricate detail. Of course, a part of Kate had always believed that Molly was exaggerating. Now after last night, Kate realized she owed her friend an apology. And her brain was jumping from one thought to another.

Her subconscious was probably doing it on purpose to keep her from focusing too much on what happened next. What was she supposed to say to Sean? How was she supposed to act?

"I smell coffee."

She whipped around to watch Sean walk into the kitchen. Her heart gave a hard thump, and Kate took a breath trying to calm that stir of something hot and wonderful that happened with a single look at him. His black hair tumbled across his forehead, his blue eyes were narrowed. He wore black jeans and a white long-sleeved shirt, unbuttoned. He hadn't bothered to pull on his boots, and Kate couldn't have said why she found the fact that he was barefoot so damn sexy. But she knew without a doubt that she was in serious trouble.

"Coffee's almost ready," she said, focusing on the job at hand rather than the gorgeous man headed toward her with a long, slow stride.

"Good. Need the caffeine." He leaned one hip against the counter and crossed his arms over the chest she wanted to stroke like a kitten. "You wore me out. Who knew once I got you out of that tool belt you'd be so…insatiable?"

Heat and memories rushed through her again, tangling together in her mind. "It was quite the surprise for me, too," she muttered.

"Re-al-ly?" He drawled that word into three syllables.

"It's not that big a deal," Kate said, snatching

up the now-ready coffeepot and pouring each of them a cup. She needed a second or two to gather thoughts she'd only been considering for the last few minutes herself. *Insatiable.* She had been. And that had surprised the heck out of her. "I just never really cared that much about sex is all."

A half smile tugged at the edge of his mouth. "But you have such a talent for it." He paused thoughtfully, then asked, "So it must be that your former lovers weren't very good."

Kate snapped a look at him. It was one thing for her to reconsider the intimacies of her marriage, but she wouldn't stand there and let Sean insult Sam's memory. "He was just fine, thanks."

"Just fine?" Sean laughed shortly, took a sip of his coffee and said, "*Fine* is not a word you want to use about sex. Cookies maybe, but not sex." He stopped, straightened up and looked at her in disbelief. "Wait a minute. You said *he*. You've only been with one other guy?"

A new tidal wave of guilt roared over her, making Kate think she'd drown in that dark, dismal sea. Yes, before Sean she'd only been with her husband. Sam's smiling face rose up in her mind and Kate's heart ached. She couldn't talk about him with Sean. Didn't want to hear sympathetic noises or see a sheen of pity in his eyes. Kate didn't even talk about Sam with her friends or her father, so she wouldn't consider it with Sean. She was dealing with Sam's loss, but she was doing it her own way. "I don't think we need to discuss our pasts. Unless you've got something you'd like to share…"

It was gone so quickly, Kate couldn't be sure she'd seen it at all. But there was a flicker of something dark in his eyes. Apparently, he was as protective of his own memories as she was of her own. Well, good, then he would understand.

"No," he finally said, "we don't have to talk about the past."

Relieved, Kate nodded. "In that case, why don't we talk about the future instead?"

In a blink, his features went stiff and tight, his eyes glittered wildly with a typical sort of blind, male panic. "What future?"

Laughter shot from her throat, startling her and

making Sean scowl in response. His expression only made her laugh harder and boy, it felt good to let go of the guilt, the awkwardness and the morning-after conversation.

"What's so damn funny?" he demanded.

Still laughing, Kate held one hand up in a silent request for time to get herself under control. Sean waited, but he wasn't happy, as evidenced by his scowl deepening.

Shaking her head, Kate realized that for the first time since awakening in Sean's arms, she felt like herself. Nerves were gone, that odd sense of guilt mingled with regret had faded away and she remembered exactly who she was. She didn't have to walk on eggshells around Sean because they weren't in a *relationship*, so to speak. They were each strong individuals and as long as she kept that in mind, she could handle whatever came next.

Laughter, though, continued to spill from her in a long, rich torrent until she struggled to catch her breath. Looking at Sean didn't help because he looked so…irritated. Men were just amazing, she told herself, amusement continuing to bubble in her mind.

Sean was a prime example. He'd done everything he could to get her into bed…well, sleeping bag. Then the following morning, all she had to do was say the word *future* and she could practically *hear* him stepping on the metaphorical brakes. She was only surprised he hadn't tried to leave—blizzard or no blizzard. He was no doubt assuming she had visions filled with white picket fences and rosy-cheeked children. Her laughter faded away as she recalled that she'd had those very dreams once. And then they died. She had no interest in resuscitating them.

When she had the laughter under control, she said, "Relax, Sean. I'm not expecting a proposal and a vow of eternal devotion. God, you should see your face. You look like you're ready to chew off a cartoon ball and chain from around your ankle."

"That's ridiculous." If anything, his frown deepened as he took a long drink of coffee. "And I don't know what you're talking about."

"Sure," she said, shaking her head as she sipped at her coffee. "You stick with that. Anyway…I was talking about the hotel's future, not ours."

He stiffened and pushed away from the counter with a move that was too studiedly casual to be real. "I knew that."

"Please." She laughed again, waved that away and took another hit of her coffee. "When you walked in here, you were braced for some emotional meltdown from me. You figured I'd throw myself at your feet and beg you to marry me or some weird thing."

"Weird?" His eyebrows lifted.

"Well, you have no worries on that front," she assured him, meeting those icy blue eyes squarely. "I'm not interested in a husband and if I was, it wouldn't be *you*."

He just looked at her for a long minute before blurting, "What the hell's wrong with me?"

Kate laughed again. "Wow. Now you're insulted."

"No. Yeah. I guess I am. Why wouldn't you want to marry me?"

"Let's see," she said thoughtfully, tipping her head to one side to look up at him. "For one thing, your first thought was to bolt out of the room when you thought I might be swooning over you."

"I wouldn't bolt," he told her stiffly. "It's snowing."

"Uh-huh. For another, you're irritating."

"Ha!" He flashed a quick grin. "Hello, pot? This is kettle. You're black."

"Funny," she admitted. "Fine. We irritate each other. Good enough reason to steer clear. Another is the fact that you're California and I'm Wyoming. Not exactly geographically desirable. And then there's the fact that anytime I see you in some magazine, you've got a hot blonde with boobs bigger than her IQ on your arm."

"That's sexist," he pointed out wryly.

"I'm a woman. I can say it," she said. "Face it, Sean. You're just not marriage material. You don't want a permanent woman and I have no use for a permanent man, so why on earth would I want to marry you?"

He looked at her for a long moment, then set down his coffee cup and reached for her. She went willingly enough because hey, Kate already knew how amazing he could make her feel.

"All very logical," he said, nodding. "Good points, too. But you left one thing out."

"Yeah? What's that?"

"Sex," he said with a shrug. "Between us, it's incredible."

"Not enough to build a marriage on and why are we still talking about this?" she asked.

"Because I want you to admit you want me."

"I do—just not as a husband."

"I can live with that," he said, one corner of his amazing mouth tipping up into a smile that tugged at something deep inside her. Kate felt herself melting. Sean Ryan was so bad for her. Maybe that's why she was enjoying him so much.

His gaze fixed on her mouth, and she licked her lips in anticipation. When he bent his head and kissed her, she sank into it. This thing between them was powerful, energizing, and she would be a fool not to take everything she could from this interlude before her world went back to normal.

A few hours later, the memory of Kate's laughter was sharp and bright in Sean's mind. He hated knowing that she'd been right about his reaction when she talked about a future. It was knee-jerk for most men, probably. They were, as a species, fairly suspicious, waiting for a woman to get that white-picket-fence gleam in her eye. A man had to stay wary just to make sure he had time to make a clean getaway.

Sean had had it happen to him too many times to count. Every casual relationship he'd ever been in had eventually become a tug-of-war centered around marriage. He knew what the women were thinking—a wedding. Kids. Access to Sean Ryan's fortune. Was it so surprising then that he immediately assumed that Kate was no different?

But, of course, she was, he told himself grimly. Not only was she not interested in snagging him into some kind of relationship, but she also found the very idea laughable and that just annoyed hell out of him.

"The snow's getting to you," he muttered. It was the only explanation, Sean thought. "Being trapped with a woman like Kate is bound to make a man a little nuts."

She was like no one he'd ever known. She filled his thoughts, tormented his body and, at the moment, was working him like a slave driver. Sean was used to running meetings, winning over clients and snagging huge market deals. He had meetings. Dinners. Drinks with a client at some exclusive restaurant.

What he wasn't accustomed to was swinging a hammer. He'd already helped her pull up linoleum in one bathroom, tear down some hideous paneling in what would eventually be the first-floor game room and now he'd been tasked to tear up some—God help him—*shag* carpeting in one of the upstairs suites. He tightened his grip on the worn, wooden handle, slid the claw top beneath the edge of the faded floor covering and pried it loose.

Carpet tacks gave, and Sean tossed the hammer aside to grab the rug with both hands. He pulled it up as he backed across the room and coughed at the years of dust flying into the air. It was hard, dirty work, and he was getting a new appreciation for the men and women who did this kind of thing daily.

Women like Kate. When he first met her a week ago, Sean had seen only the coldly efficient shell of the woman. She knew her job and wasn't afraid to stand up to Sean when she believed she was right. He'd admired that even while arguing with her.

Now he knew more. Knew the heat of her, the passion bubbling right beneath the surface. Knew that even while she gave herself to him, she kept parts of herself locked away. It surprised him to realize how much he wanted to know what she was hiding. And why. She would close him out expertly at the slightest threat of getting too close.

*Like you?* his mind whispered.

Scowling, he told himself that everyone had

secrets. Everyone had pockets of regret or guilt or misery tucked away that were rarely brought out to be inspected. His were his own business— hell, even Mike didn't know about them—and so he would leave Kate with hers.

What lay between them was desire born of convenience. That was it. So he'd work, he'd sleep with her and then when they finally got the hell out of this damned hotel, he'd go home. Where he belonged and where he could put this whole situation into perspective.

"Nice job."

She moved quietly. He turned to look at Kate, standing in the open doorway. Sean didn't want to admit, even to himself, what seeing her wearing a damn tool belt did to him. She looked confident and too damned sexy for his peace of mind. Her worn jeans hugged her legs, the hem of her tunic sweater hung to her hips and her boots were as scarred as his own. The tool belt that was currently driving him insane fit her as undeniably as diamonds might another woman.

Man, he was losing it fast.

"Thanks," he said wryly. "But pulling up old carpet doesn't take a lot of finesse."

"Just time and effort," she agreed, then walked into the room and skirted around him and the roll of carpet. She went down to one knee to examine the wood floor that had been hidden beneath the ratty carpet. "Looks good," she mused, more to herself than to him. "I was hoping for this. Hardwood, even battered and scarred like this, can be sanded and brought back to life a lot cheaper than buying new floors throughout."

Nodding, he watched her stroke her fingertips over the wide planks with the same gentleness she'd used to caress his chest. His body stirred, and he gritted his teeth, ignoring the flash of heat.

She whipped her ponytail back out of her way and glanced at him. "If all the floors look this good, we'll be saving you a lot of money."

"Always a good thing," he agreed.

She stood. "I've got the rugs in two other rooms rolled up and their floors are nearly perfect, so

I'm hopeful. What I'd like to do now is check out the basement, see what we've got down there."

"Didn't you already do that when you made your first inspection for your bid on the job?"

"Sure." She shrugged and rested one hand on the hammer hanging from her belt. "But it was a quick look, mainly checking for foundation issues. Now that we've got some time…"

He laughed shortly. "Plenty of that."

"Exactly. We can look at it and see what improvements can be made."

One eyebrow winged up. "We're done pulling up carpet?"

"I just wanted to get an idea of the shape of the floors. The rest my crew can do when the storm's over."

One glance at the window told Sean the snow was still swirling like a thick white veil. "If it's ever over."

"It will be. I've been through these storms all my life."

"Not me," he said with a sigh born of missing

the ocean, the sand, the sea breeze. "I'm a surf-and-sand kind of guy."

"You'll be back to it soon," she told him, and their gazes locked for one tension-filled moment. "For now, though…the basement?"

"Why not?" He shrugged, following her as she headed downstairs, and his gaze dropped unerringly to the curve of her behind. Whatever else the woman was, she had a great butt and the ability to work him into an inferno without even trying. He had to admire that even while it made him a little crazy.

"The banisters will have to be tightened," she said over her shoulder. "The base is loose and you don't want it wobbly."

"Absolutely not." He gave said banister a shake and felt it wiggle under his hand. Right again, he thought, then told himself this was why he'd hired her in the first place. Kate Wells had a reputation for being a perfectionist when it came to her work, and that was something he understood and approved of.

She hit the bottom of the stairs and headed

across the great room, where the fire still burned against the constant chill in the room. Through the kitchen and into the butler's pantry, she opened the door to the basement and started down the stairs.

The light spilled from two overhead lamps, illuminating a wide room that was empty but for a line of dated washing machines and dryers. There was a workbench along one wall and a pegboard above it, just waiting for someone to fill it with tools. The floor was cement, the windows were narrow and high, blocked now with piles of snow. The walls were cement blocks, which only seemed to magnify the cold outside the building.

"I always thought basements were a little creepy," Sean said to himself.

"Agreed," Kate said, throwing him a quick look as she pulled out a measuring tape and laid it down on the floor as she walked off the space. "But they don't have to be. Still, having the laundry down here doesn't seem real handy for the housekeeping staff." She paused to make note of numbers on a small memo pad she dug out of her tool belt. "Especially since they have to come and go through the kitchen."

"You're right." Nodding, he glanced back up the stairs before reluctantly admitting, "I wouldn't have thought of that. But if the kitchen staff is busy, then having housekeeping coming and going will make everyone's job harder than it has to be."

She made a few more notations, then wound the tape back into its shell. With it tucked away, she inspected the block walls and said, "A little insulation down here would make it more livable."

"Another good idea," he said. "Do it."

"That was easy." She looked at him. "And since you're being so reasonable, what do you think about moving the laundry facilities to the old owner's suite? It's on the other side of the hotel, opposite the great room, and there's plenty of space for water and electrical hookup, plus worktables for the folding or ironing or whatever is needed."

Sean pulled the layout of the hotel into his mind and could see it just as she'd described it.

"Yeah, that'd work. Be easier for everyone. But then we've got an empty basement and don't really need the insulation, do we?"

"Of course we do," she argued neatly. "Insulating down here will help keep the floors above warmer, cutting down on heating bills. And you could set this up as a tool room for the maintenance crew you'll need to hire."

He walked down the rest of the steps, stopped beside her and laughed shortly. "And they *won't* get in the way upstairs in the kitchen."

"Nope," she told him before walking across the room to slap one hand against the wall. "Because we'll cut out a double door right here, with a ramp, so maintenance can get heavy tools and machinery in and out with no problem. Gives them easy access to what they need, and you know you'll need riding mowers and at least a couple of snowblowers, as well. They can be stored down here. There's plenty of space for everything you could ever need."

He could see it once she'd painted the picture, and Sean was only a little annoyed that he hadn't seen it before. But why would he? He'd never used a snowblower in his life and since he lived in a condo at the beach, he really didn't need a lawn mower, either, did he?

Unaccustomed to having to work out solutions for anything other than how to market their next video game, he was stumbling around in the dark here. And all in all, he thought he was doing a pretty damn good job of it.

"Okay, it's a good plan."

She just looked at him for a long moment, then cocked her head and asked, "Why are you being so agreeable all of a sudden? We spent the first week you were in Wyoming arguing about everything."

She had a point there, too. But from the first, she'd gotten under his skin. Sean hadn't wanted to admit it was desire chewing at his insides, so instead he'd told himself her attitude was aggravating. Maybe she'd had some great ideas all along and he'd just been too distracted by what she did to him to hear her out. And that knowledge was lowering for a man who had always prided himself on his ability to focus.

"Things change," he finally said.

"I guess that's true enough." She came toward him, but instead of stopping alongside him, she walked past and took the stairs back up to the main floor.

"What're you doing now?"

She stopped in the threshold and was backlit by the kitchen light. Her face in shadows, he felt her smile more than he could see it. "As long as you're in such a good mood," she said, "I figured we could start tearing down one of the walls to check the wiring."

He choked out a laugh. "Seriously?"

"Okay, not the whole wall, but we should be able to at least rip away enough drywall to take a peek."

"And you want to do construction while we're trapped in a blizzard, why?"

"We can't stay in bed all day," she said.

His body burned at the thought. "Don't see why not."

"Of course you don't. And what you and I will be doing upstairs is not construction," she insisted, flipping her ponytail behind her. "It's more *de*-struction. What we in the building business lovingly call 'demo day.'"

"Great. Demo."

"Come on. You'll like it."

Well, he told himself as he climbed the stairs, if they weren't going to be having sex, at least he could take out his frustrations with a hammer.

# Five

They worked together all day, with Kate keeping them too busy and occupied for either of them to consider heading back to the sleeping bag. Though the temptation of it nibbled at her continuously. How could she not think of it? Sean had opened up a world of sensations she'd never expected. And she wanted to feel them all again in spite of the fact that her mind kept warning her off. Logically, her mind was absolutely right and her body should take a time-out.

The problem was, what she was feeling had nothing to do with logic. When the day finally ended and the snow was still falling, she was out of distractions. They shared another meal from their dwindling supplies and when they were finished, Sean reached for her and she went to him. Knowing it was a mistake to continue doing what she knew she shouldn't, Kate still couldn't stop herself. There was so much to be discovered in his arms, and she wanted—needed—to know everything.

But sometime during the night, the snow finally stopped. By morning, the sky was a brilliant blue and the sunshine on all the fresh snow shone like diamonds under a spotlight. Kate should have been relieved, happy that this forced togetherness was at an end. Instead, she really wasn't.

"How long do you think it'll take for the pass to be cleared?" Sean asked.

She glanced at him standing beside her at the wall of windows in the great room. "A few hours. The county plows will get to it fast."

"Then all we'll have to do is dig out the driveway so we can get your truck out of the garage."

"We won't have to." She smiled to herself and

shook her head. "Now that the storm's over, I'll call one of my crew. Raul's got a snow blade for his pickup. He makes extra cash plowing mountain roads for residents. He can get up here to clear this as soon as the county's done with the pass."

"So we're almost free," he mused quietly.

"Yep," she quipped, hoping for a light tone that would hide the yawning pit of emptiness opening up inside her. "Your nightmare ends today."

He took her arm, turned her to face him and when she did, his gaze moved over her face like a touch. "I wouldn't say nightmare."

She wished she could read his eyes, see what he was thinking, but whatever he was feeling was carefully masked. "No?"

He shook his head. "Let's think of it as a three-day seminar. Sean and Kate 101."

In spite of everything, a tiny chuckle escaped her. She had learned a lot about Sean. Maybe too much, but it was too late to go back and *un*-learn it even if she wanted to. "And now class is over."

"Almost." He moved in, set his hands at her

waist and effortlessly lifted her against him until she had no choice but to hook her legs around his hips. He stared into her eyes, then gave her a slow, wicked smile. "I think we have time for one more recess."

God, he really *was* charming, she thought. She stared into those lake-blue eyes of his and knew that when he was gone, she was going to miss him. She didn't want to. She'd like to go back to her old life and leave these few days with Sean in the past, where they belonged. But that, she realized now, would be impossible.

He'd touched more than her body during their time together. He'd reached into her heart and brought it back to life again. And with that life she knew there would be pain. But for now, there was still joy to be found.

"Exercise is important," she said.

"There you go."

Two days later, Sean was back in California. He deliberately jumped back into his real life, diving into the plans and strategies for launching their next video game, "The Wild Hunt," in early summer. While he talked to distributors, marketing and the Celtic Knot website division, he was able to push thoughts of Kate out of his mind. He buried himself in work until the memory of a snowbound hotel and a tiny, gorgeous woman with a pit-bull attitude were nothing more than misty images nibbling at his brain. Which was just the way he liked it, he assured himself. His focus was on the job, where it belonged. Wyoming was a long way from Long Beach, California.

Just as well. Despite the snow and the cold and the fact that they had lived on coffee, shared sandwiches, cookies and crackers, Sean had been getting way too comfortable in that drafty old hotel. Nights spent with Kate in his arms, waking up with her sprawled across his body while a roaring fire hissed and crackled in the stillness was just too...*something*, he told himself, not really wanting to identify the feeling any more than that. Being there with her had confused the situation. Getting back to their own lives and their own work were the only real answers for either of them.

So why, then, was he in such a crappy mood? He'd already snapped at Linda, their admin, rejected their lead artist's idea for the upcoming Christmas game and managed to insult one of their biggest clients. And it wasn't even noon.

"There something you want to talk about, Sean?"

"What?" He looked up and saw his brother, Mike, standing in the open doorway of Sean's office. "No." He picked up a sheaf of papers and rattled them for emphasis. "Busy here."

"Yeah," Mike said, walking into the room and dropping into the visitor's chair opposite Sean. "Me, too. So let's wade through all of the denials and get down to whatever it is that's got your shorts in a knot."

Family could be a real pain. Especially an older brother who saw too much and knew you too well. Shooting that brother a dirty look, Sean asked, "When did you get so insightful all of a sudden?"

"When Dave tells me you eighty-sixed the sketch of the Nightmare Pooka. Linda was crying at her desk. And oh, yeah, Dexter Stevens called to complain about your attitude."

"That's rich," Sean muttered, deliberately refusing to pick up the gauntlet of guilt Mike was tossing him. "Dave's drawing was mediocre at best—"

"Preliminary sketch," Mike added.

"Since Linda got pregnant, she cries when the phone rings—"

"And so she doesn't need *you* giving her more to be upset about," Mike interrupted.

"As for Dexter," Sean continued as if his brother hadn't spoken at all, "he's given us plenty of grief over the last two years, and we've never called him on it."

"Yeah," Mike said, "because his distribution network moved almost two million units of 'Fate Castle.'"

Sean frowned, remembering their first major best seller game. All right, Mike had a point there. Dexter had given the beta version of the game to his teenage sons, and they'd loved it. With their recommendation, Dexter's company had covered the entire northeastern portion of the country with "Fate Castle" at a substantial discount that had pushed Celtic Knot up to the next level. Was Dexter a jerk personally? Sure. But he was also hell on wheels at distribution, and they couldn't afford to offend him.

In self-defense, though, Sean scrubbed one hand across his face and blew out a breath. "Dexter Stevens is a pain in the—"

"And has been for years," Mike said, cutting him off. "Still no reason to give one of our best partners such a hard time."

He was right, but Sean didn't want to admit it. His first day back at work, and he was making everyone as miserable as he was. Upside to this situation? Dexter would be fine once Sean apologized—which he would do as soon as he could get Mike out of his office.

Normally, dealing with their suppliers, clients and distributors was something Sean enjoyed. He liked people and figuring out how to work with the different personalities he encountered. But today, he simply hadn't had the patience to deal with Dexter, and that was his own fault.

"Yeah," Sean muttered. "I'll call him later. Offer to send him an early version of 'The Wild Hunt' for his kids."

"Great. So want to tell me what's going on with you?"

"Nothing. Everything's good." Sean sat back, kicked his feet up to the corner of his desk and folded his hands on his abdomen. The casual stance didn't fool his brother.

"Sell that to someone who doesn't know you." Mike cocked his head to study Sean. "Things were fine before you got snowed in. So. Want to tell me what happened in the hotel between you and Kate?"

That'd be the day. Hell, looking back at it all from a safe distance, even *he* wasn't sure what had happened between him and Kate. And he was really trying not to think about any of it. So, instead of answering, Sean asked a question of his own. "Want to tell me what's going on between you and Jenny?"

For some reason, Mike and Jenny Marshall, one of the artists at Celtic Knot, got along as well as a lit match and a stick of dynamite. But Sean had the distinct impression something was going on between them. His first clue was the way Mike went cold and silent the minute Jenny's name was mentioned. Like now, for instance.

Instantly, Mike's features tightened and his eyes shuttered. *Ha*, Sean thought. *Not so much fun prying when it's your secrets being uncovered, is it?*

"Jenny's doing a good job at the Laughlin hotel."

"Uh-huh. Nice stall and, hey, extra points for evasion," Sean said with a knowing smile. "What's she doing to *you*?"

Mike's eyes narrowed, and he pushed himself to his feet. "Fine," he said tightly. "You made your point. You don't want to talk about Kate and I don't want to talk about Jenny, so let all of this rest and get back to work."

Satisfied, Sean nodded. "Sounds like a plan."

Mike headed for the door but stopped long enough to add, "And don't piss off any more of our clients, okay?"

When he was alone again, Sean swiveled his chair around to look out the window at the backyard. The majestic old Victorian mansion where Celtic Knot made its offices sat on Pacific Coast Highway. Just across the wide, busy street, the ocean stretched out to the horizon and from the back of the house, the view was a large, neatly tended yard. Of course now, in the middle of a Southern California winter, the grass was brown and the gardens desolate but for a few lingering chrysanthemums. Overhead, the sky was clear with white clouds scudding along like sailboats on an endless sea. He was a long way from Wyoming, Sean told himself.

So why was he daydreaming about snow?

It was snowing again.

Kate listened to the Muzak coming through her phone while she was on hold and looked through the front window, watching as a thick, white blanket fell from steel-gray skies. It wasn't a blizzard—she and her crew wouldn't be snowbound here at the hotel. It was just another Wyoming winter storm, and it made her think of Sean and how only a few days ago the two of them had been alone here.

She missed him.

Kate hadn't expected that at all. He had been such an irritation at first that all she had wanted was for him to leave, go back to California. Now? She wished he was there. She ached for him, and that was hard to accept.

"Ms. Wells?"

The music ended abruptly, and Kate dragged her mind back to work. Much, much better than thinking about Sean, which wouldn't do her any good at all. "Yes. I'm here. And I'm wondering why my Dumpsters aren't."

"Well, now," the condescending male voice on the other end of the line said, "I understand you're a little impatient, but we won't be able to haul the Dumpsters through the pass for another day or two at least."

Kate gritted her teeth, took a slow, deep breath and said, "The pass is clear, Henry, and I need those Dumpsters on-site."

He chuckled, and Kate wanted to scream.

"In case you hadn't noticed, missie, it's snowing again, and we don't want to get halfway through the pass and find we can't maneuver the rest of the way."

They both knew this storm was no issue. But Kate was also aware that pushing Henry Jackson wouldn't get her anywhere. "Fine. Then I can expect them here by Friday?"

"As long as the weather holds," he said, managing to agree and not promise a thing.

"Fine. Thank you." That cost her, but Henry was the closest supplier. If she had to arrange for someone else to deliver Dumpsters, it could take twice as long. So she'd make nice for the good of the job and hope he came through. Eventually.

When she hung up, she stayed where she was until her annoyance dropped a couple of levels.

"If the snow was so bad, we wouldn't be here working, would we?" she asked herself. "The pass is clear, Henry's just lazy, which you already knew."

If the pass was still blocked, she and Sean would still be trapped here, just the two of them. A ping of something sad and sweet echoed in the center of her chest, and she absently rubbed the spot, futilely hoping to ease it. It didn't help.

"Yo, boss!"

Kate looked up, to where Raul stood at the head of the stairs. "What is it?"

"With no Dumpsters here, where do you want us to pile all the stuff we're tearing out?"

Kate scowled, glanced around the hotel, then back up to the tall man waiting for her decision. "Right now, just toss everything out a window to a clear spot in the yard. We'll load up the Dumpsters when Henry finally decides to bring them up."

"You got it."

Twice the work, twice the time, but there was nothing else to do about it. Kate figured she could do one of two things. Keep thinking about Sean and wondering what he was doing right now. Or she could get to work on this hotel and keep herself too occupied to think about the man who had so briefly lit up her world.

Grimly, she set off for the kitchen. Tearing out old cabinets ought to keep her busy enough.

Sean spent the next few weeks working on the Celtic Knot game plan. Focused, he could avoid thoughts of Wyoming and what had happened there until it was only in sleep that memories of Kate swung around to haunt him.

When he'd first returned home, he'd done his best to make images of her and those snowbound days fade from his mind by going out with other women. Lots of women. But none of them had managed to get his attention. He took them dancing, to fancy dinners and concerts, and within twenty minutes of every damn date, Sean was bored and his mind was drifting. After a few weeks, he stopped trying. Just wasn't worth the effort. He figured it was a sign from the universe, telling him to forget about *all* women for a while and concentrate on his company. Sooner or later, he'd get back to decorating his bed with beautiful women. Until then, he poured what concentration he could find into the work.

He was still talking to companies about making a set of collectible figures based on the characters from some of their biggest games. He was also in talks about developing a board game based on "Fate Castle" to capture the imaginations of those few people who preferred their games in the real world rather than the digital one.

Then there were the storyboards to go over, checking out the dialogue and scene shots for their upcoming Christmas release, and that didn't take into account setting the groundwork for the first Celtic Knot convention—along the lines of the big fantasy cons, but set solely around the Celtic Knot video games.

The Wyoming hotel was their only holding big enough to accommodate a con of any kind and now that Sean had both Mike and their partner,

Brady Finn, on board with the idea, Sean had to get things rolling.

That meant, whether he wanted to or not, he had to talk to Kate about it. The fact that there was a part of him looking forward to seeing her face again was something he didn't want to think about. Over the last several weeks, they'd communicated mostly through email, except for one phone call that had been brief and unsatisfying. Hearing her voice had sparked his memories even as the distance between them had sharpened the frustration gnawing at him.

His cell phone beeped, and he glanced at it. Today would be a video chat, and he wasn't at all sure if it would be better or worse to actually see her face when he spoke to her. On the second beep, he grabbed it and answered. Kate's face popped up on the screen, and he felt a jolt of something that was part pleasure, part irritation. Why'd she have to look so damn good?

"Kate," he said tightly. "Good to see you."

"Hello, Sean." She paused as if she was considering what to say, so he spoke up to fill the void.

"I wanted to talk to you about plans for the conventions we'll want to hold at the hotel."

"Right." She nodded. "You told me a little about your plans when you were here."

"Yeah." Her eyes were direct, and so blue he felt as though he could fall into them and drown. Not easy to keep your mind on work when you were looking into those eyes, he told himself. "It's why we're going to need those extra cabins."

"Oh," she said, perking up, "I wanted to talk to you about the cabins, too."

"Okay, but first tell me how much progress you're making." Because while she talked he could enjoy watching her. The flicker of emotion on her face, the shine in her eyes, the way her mouth moved…

"Well," she said, "the interior work is going great. We've got most of the kitchen finished, and the quartz counters will be going in by the end of the week…"

She kept talking, detailing the work being done, and he knew he should be more focused on it. He, his brother and Brady Finn had each been in charge of a hotel's makeover, turning them into exact replicas of one of their bestselling games.

Fans all over the world were already lining up to stay in "Fate Castle" in Ireland, where Brady lived, and the Laughlin hotel based on the "River Haunt" game was next, probably opening around Christmas in conjunction with the latest game being released. Then there was this one.

Sean's hotel was based on "Forest Run," a game featuring soulless creatures, brave knights, sorcerers and Faery warriors. This hotel strategy was important, as it offered their gamers the chance to live out the fantasies of the games. It was one of the next big steps Celtic Knot was taking to push them into the stratosphere of success.

So yeah, Sean should be listening, making notes, but instead, all he saw were Kate's eyes, and he remembered how they looked with fire-light dancing in their depths. He saw her mouth moving and nearly felt the soft glide of her kisses across his chest. She flipped her ponytail back over her shoulder, but he saw a thick mass of soft black hair spilling around her face as she rode him to completion.

"So, what do you think?"

"What?" His brain tried to catch up. To sift through what she'd said to pick out a few key words so he wouldn't have to admit he hadn't been listening. "The cottages?"

She rolled her beautiful eyes. "Yeah. What do you think about the new idea for their design?"

*Stall*, he told himself. *Use that charm you're always insisting you have.* "Well, it's not easy to make a decision without more than just a description."

Her eyes narrowed on him. "Yeah, I thought you'd say that. So I had my friend Molly draw these up. She's not one of your artists, but she's better at it than I am." She held up a tablet and showed him a raw, rough sketch. Intrigued, he brought the phone closer to examine what she was showing him. His first reaction was that he liked the idea very much.

Instead of a squat, square cabin as they'd first

discussed, she'd come up with something that would look...almost mystical.

"It's sort of based on caravan wagons," she was saying as she flipped pages to show him more.

He could see the inspiration behind the drawings. The cabins themselves looked like half circles, resting on the flat edge. Walls and roofs curved with arched doorways brought to mind fantasy houses from fairy stories. Each one would be singular, individual, he saw, as he studied the different drawings. He could see it, the small, rounded cabins nestled in the forest, surrounded by flowers and trees, their brightly colored doors signaling welcome. Hell, he thought, people would stand in line to stay in those cabins.

When she was finished and faced him on the screen again, she asked, "So? Shall we go with these? I'm asking now because the ground's getting soft enough to start excavation. We'll have to install a new septic system, centrally located so we can connect all the cabins to it. Once that's in, we'd like to lay foundations for the cabins themselves."

"Septic system," he repeated with a short laugh.

"Well, yeah," she said. "We're too far from the county sewer lines to hook into them, and the hotel's tank isn't big enough to handle the extra load from the cabins."

He chuckled again and pushed one hand through his hair.

"What's so funny?"

"This conversation," he told her. "I don't think I've ever discussed sewers with a lover before."

"Ex-lover," she amended quickly.

A ping of something sharp and cold shot through him, but he let it pass. "Point taken. Okay, yeah. I like the drawings a lot. Make sure you leave the walls blank for our artists to come in and paint murals based on the game."

"Right," she said, all business again. "We're on that. And in the hotel, we've got acres of white walls just waiting for them. I think we should wait until most of the work's done before you send anyone out, though."

"Agreed." He turned his chair until he was facing the window with a view of the backyard and the flowers beginning to bloom there. Spring was coming, and he wondered if all the snow at the hotel had melted yet. Not the point, he reminded himself. "Fax me those sketches, will you? I want to show them to Mike and the artists. Run them past an architect and get some plans. They'll probably need refining, too."

"I'll send them this afternoon."

"Okay," Sean said and wanted to ask how she was.

"Then, I guess that's it." She looked over her shoulder and it wasn't until then that Sean keyed into the background noise of hammers and saws. "I should get back to work."

"Yeah," he said. "Me, too."

"So, good," she said, nodding. "Everything's good. I'll keep you posted with emails about the progress here."

"That'll work." His gaze locked onto her face even though he knew that seeing her like this would only feed the dreams that were already tormenting him nightly. That fact annoyed him, so his voice was brusquer than he'd intended when he said, "I'll expect those faxes today."

"You'll have them. Look," she said, "I've gotta go."

"Yeah, me, too," he said again and noticed that neither one of them was making a move to hang up. Were they twelve? That spurred him to action. "All right. Thanks for checking in and for the suggestions."

"You're welcome. Bye." And she was gone.

In the sudden silence of his empty office, Sean felt a chill far deeper than he'd experienced in a snowbound hotel.

# Six

*Five months later*

His brother was married.

Sean was having a hard time getting his head around it, but facts were facts. Jenny Marshall was now Jenny Ryan—a new bride and pregnant with their first child. The baby had been a surprise and had really knocked Mike off his game for a while. But he'd come around, worked out his own issues and finally realized in time that Jenny was the only woman for him.

The Balboa Pavilion was the perfect spot for

a summer wedding, too. He glanced around at the stately old Victorian, with its wide view of Newport Bay and the hundreds of pleasure crafts lining the docks. The dance floor was gleaming beneath thousands of tiny white lights and beyond the glass walls, a summer moon shone down on it all as if in celebration.

Sean's gaze shifted back to where his brother and Jenny were dancing, holding each other as if they were the only two people in the world. Times change, Sean told himself as he leaned negligently against a wall. Not too long ago, Mike and Jenny had been at each other's throats. Now they were pledging eternal love and about to be parents. Speaking of parents... Sean turned his head to look at his own folks. Jack and Peggy Ryan looked as happy as he'd ever seen them. He frowned thoughtfully and took a sip of the aged Scotch in his hand.

His parents' marriage had always seemed pretty damn perfect to Sean. It was only recently that he'd learned what Mike had discovered at the tender age of thirteen—that parents were people who made mistakes. It still didn't sit well with him that Mike had kept the secret of the trouble in their parents' marriage to himself for so many years. But on the other hand, Sean mused as he watched his mom lean her head on his dad's shoulder, Sean had secrets of his own.

He'd never actually lied to the family about anything, but he'd never told them everything, either. So he really wasn't in a position to complain too loud or too long.

But this wasn't the time to think about the past. This was about Mike and Jenny, who had somehow gone from antagonism to the kind of love most people never knew.

Naturally, thinking about antagonists brought him around to thoughts of Kate. But to be honest, his mind was always ready to dredge up Kate's image. Five months and he could still smell her. Taste her. Her face swam in his mind every night when he tried to sleep. It wasn't getting better. If anything, his brain seemed to be working overtime reminding him about Kate, as if to ensure he didn't forget.

As if he could. Memories of their days and nights together kept his body at a slow burn constantly. Maybe, he told himself, it was time to go back to Wyoming. Check on the hotel's progress in person rather than reading about it in faxed reports and sterile emails. And while he was at it, he could see Kate again and resolve whatever the hell was gnawing at him. He had no doubt that his memories were playing with him, convincing him that Kate was more than she really was. Making the memories of the incredible, breathtaking sex they'd shared wildly better than the reality. Seeing her again could clear up all of that. Help him put things in perspective so he could finally get her the hell out of his head.

With that thought in mind, he stepped away from the music and the crowd, pulled his cell phone out of his pocket and hit the number for a video chat. After a couple of rings, she answered and the instant her face appeared on the screen, his body tightened in response.

What was it about this one woman?

"Sean?" She didn't look happy to see him. Her

eyes narrowed and she bit at her bottom lip before saying, "I wasn't expecting to hear from you." She glanced away, then back, as if she was reluctant to meet his eyes. "We're, um, kind of busy here. Is there a problem?"

He hadn't thought so, but he was changing his mind fast. Whatever else Kate was, she wasn't a game player. And judging by her expression right now, she shouldn't play poker.

"You tell me," he said, moving farther from the festivities so he could hear her better. He left the Pavilion and stepped out into the summer night, where the music from inside was muffled and the slap of water against the dock sounded like a heartbeat. "Something wrong?"

"No," she assured him quickly. "Everything's fine. Great, really. Uh, what's all the music I hear?"

"My brother, Mike, just got married. I'm at the reception."

"Oh, that's nice." She bit her lip again. "Um, I'm a little busy, Sean."

Anxious. Why?

"Yeah," he said shortly. "Me, too, so why don't you save us both some time and tell me what's going on?"

She took a breath and impatiently huffed it out again. "Fine. We're making serious progress on the hotel and—"

She kept talking, but Sean was hardly listening. Instead he watched her face and studied the secrecy shining in her eyes. There was something going on, and she clearly didn't want to talk to him about it. If it was job related, she wouldn't have a problem. He already knew that Kate took her work as seriously as he took his. She was on schedule with the remodel, so what the hell was it that could make her so clearly uneasy about talking to him? Did she have a new man in her life?

Sean really didn't like that thought. Gritting his teeth, he interrupted her rapid flow of words with one sharp question. "Why are you so nervous about talking to me?"

"Nervous?" She forced a laugh, then shook her head so hard her ponytail swung like a pendulum behind her head. "I'm not nervous, Sean.

Just busy. We're at a critical stage in the job, and I should be out supervising the concrete pour for the cabin foundations. I really don't have time for this, Sean."

"Is that right?" His voice was cool, distant, but she didn't seem to notice.

She smiled, but it didn't touch the shadows in her eyes. "Absolutely. I appreciate you checking in, but everything's good. I'll contact you next week. You should really go enjoy the wedding."

"Uh-huh."

"Sorry, one of my guys is calling for me. Gotta run." Then she hung up.

Sean was left staring at his phone while behind him, music, laughter and celebration rang out. She was lying. Or if not lying then at least hiding something. The question was *what*? And *why*? Scowling, he slipped the phone back into his pocket and turned to head back into the reception. The temper he hadn't really experienced since the last time he was with Kate was back now. She had *hung up on him*. Nobody did that to Sean Ryan.

The damn woman was apparently *still* convinced that she was in charge. Giving him the brush-off? Saying she was too busy to talk to him? Yeah, that wasn't going to fly.

He turned his gaze out to the dance floor, where his brother was dancing with their mom and Jenny was dancing with her uncle Hank. And while he watched everyone, his mind was at work. After the party, Mike and Jenny were heading out for a weeklong honeymoon. The minute they got back, Sean told himself, he'd be taking another trip to Wyoming to check out the situation for himself.

"Let's see her avoid me when I'm standing right in front of her," he muttered.

"Why don't I ever get snowbound with a gorgeous bazillionaire?" Molly Feeney plopped into one of Kate's comfy chairs and picked up her wineglass from the nearby table.

"Because you're lucky?" Kate asked.

"Please." Molly took a sip of her chardonnay and said, "Women around the world would have *loved* to be snowbound with Sean Ryan. He's..." She paused and slapped one hand to her heart. "I'm feeling a little faint."

Kate laughed at the drama. "That's because you haven't met him."

"You could fix that and introduce me," Molly said.

"I like you too much," Kate told her.

Laughing, Molly said, "Come on. It's not like he's an ogre."

No, he wasn't. This would all be so much easier if he was. Instead, he was as charming as he claimed to be, along with irritating, funny, frustrating. He made her feel too many things at once, which was just one reason why she should be grateful he'd gone back home to California. Having several hundred miles between them seemed much safer to Kate.

"Molly, those three days in the hotel changed everything for me," Kate mused, grabbing her tea for a long drink.

"You don't seem to be suffering for it, though," Molly pointed out with a smile.

"No, I'm not," Kate said. Suffering, no. Worrying? You bet. Along with guilt and too many other wildly divergent emotions to even consider listing.

When Sean first left Wyoming, it had been hard. She'd gotten accustomed to seeing him every day, having him challenge her both on the job and personally. She'd thought her life would be easier once he was gone. She hadn't expected to miss him, hadn't wanted to admit even to herself how deeply he'd gotten to her. But the truth was difficult to ignore, and lying to yourself never did any good because you knew the truth no matter what you told yourself. *And now I'm officially rambling.*

"Maybe if you weren't hiding…" Molly cradled her wineglass between her palms.

"Don't start." Kate shook her head and frowned at her very best friend. Molly had been dogging her about this for months. Heck, so had Kate's father, for that matter. But no matter what anyone had to say, she knew what she was doing. She'd made a decision, and she was sticking to it. "I'm doing the right thing."

Hadn't she dreamed of this very situation for years? When Sam died, Kate had accepted that those dreams were gone. Now, she had a chance to grab hold of them, and she wouldn't let it go.

"Right for who?" Molly asked, tipping her head to one side until her long, strawberry blond hair fell in a curtain of curls.

"For me. For Sean." She paused, thought about it, then nodded for emphasis. "For everyone."

"Your life, sweetie," Molly said. "And God knows I hate to interfere—"

Kate snorted.

Molly's eyebrows arched. "*But* secrets are hard to keep. The truth will eventually jump up and bite you in the butt at the worst possible time."

Kate didn't want to believe that, so she made a joke instead. "Is that a sort of variation on Murphy's Law?"

"I'm Irish," Molly told her. "We're all about Murphy's Law and all of its subsidiaries." Sighing a little, she set down her glass on the table and braced her forearms on her knees. "At least think about it, Kate."

"Molly, I have been thinking about it. For the last five months I've pretty much done nothing else *but* think about it."

"Thinking about it with your mind closed to all possibilities but the one you want isn't really thinking, is it?"

Another quick stab of guilt. "Aren't you supposed to be on my side?"

"Oh, I am, sweetie. You know that." Molly sighed. "I'm just saying that sooner or later, all secrets are blown. And it might be better if you did it yourself. You know?"

Kate let her head fall back and her gaze fix on the heavy wood beams spanning the ceiling of her cottage-style bungalow. Her friend had a point, she knew, but it was one Kate didn't want to acknowledge. "Maybe you're right, Molly. I don't know. All I'm really sure of is I can't say anything. The gorgeous bazillionaire wouldn't be interested anyway."

"Fine. I won't say anything else about it."

Oh, she didn't believe that. Molly was like a dog with a bone, and she was very protective of her friends and family. If she thought she could help, she'd never give up. But for now, Kate sighed. "Thanks. That'd be great."

When the doorbell rang, Molly jumped up and said, "I'll get it. You stay put."

Kate sipped at her tea, heard the front door open and then heard her friend's voice go soft and flirty. "Well, hi. Where'd you come from?"

"California," a familiar, deep voice said flatly. "I'm here to see Kate Wells. Is she home?"

Stomach flipping and churning, mouth going dry as dust, Kate slowly stood up, set her teacup aside and tried to harness the wild gallop of her heartbeat. This could *not* be happening. She held her breath when Molly said, "And you are?"

"Sean Ryan."

Kate groaned and half hoped that she was having some sort of weird walking dream. If she pinched herself, maybe Sean wouldn't really be walking toward her. Molly wouldn't be behind him mouthing the word *wow*, and she herself wouldn't be wearing an old T-shirt and denim shorts.

But it wasn't a dream. Sean was right in front of her, and his gaze was locked on her belly. "You're *pregnant*?"

She dropped one hand to the swell of her baby as if to protect her from hearing her parents argue even before she was born. Instantly, she went for outrage. "Sean, what're you doing here?"

If you had no defense, she reminded herself, go for a strong offense. All those years watching football games with her dad was finally paying off.

"Seriously? That's what you have to say?" He stopped, shook his head, then shoved both hands through his hair. "Are you kidding me?"

"Um," Molly said from behind Sean, "I think I'm gonna go. Looks like you two have some talking to do—"

Kate wanted to reach out and grab hold of her friend as if she was a life preserver. But what was the point? That would only be delaying the inevitable. Sean was here. He knew the truth.

Bag open, cat out. So with absolutely no other choice, Kate told herself it was best to just put it all on the table.

"I'll call you tomorrow," Kate told her, still staring at Sean.

Sean never took his gaze from the mound of Kate's belly, so he didn't see Molly miming fanning herself because he was so hot. Okay, yes, Kate thought, Sean was truly an amazing male. But right now, it wasn't desire that was pouring through her, no matter how good it felt to see him again. Panic had the upper hand at the moment.

His blue eyes lifted to meet hers, and she saw the banked fury sizzling there. "Were you ever going to tell me?" he ground out the minute the front door shut behind Molly.

"Probably not," she admitted. "At least, not unless I absolutely had to." Kate had considered this situation from every which way for the last five months. While her child grew inside her, Kate had remembered the horrified look on Sean's face when he'd thought she was trying to trap him into something permanent. Remembered him telling her he had nothing against kids, he just had no interest in having one himself.

"Sean, don't you remember? You made a point of saying you didn't want a family. You were appalled at the thought of it. Why would I tell you about my baby?"

He took a step toward her, then stopped dead as if he was too angry to get closer. "You want to use what I said about a hypothetical situation to explain you *lying* to me for five months? Not gonna work. You should have told me, Kate. Because it's *our* baby."

Kate flushed and kept her protective hand against her belly. "Fine. Technically, you're right..."

*"Technically?"* he repeated, eyes wide.

She ignored that. God, she'd imagined this conversation a million times over the last few months, whenever her guilt would get the best of her, and she pictured what might happen if Sean found out. And in none of those imaginings had he looked this...ferocious.

"Maybe I should have told you."

He choked out a short laugh.

"But it wouldn't have changed the reality, Sean. The fact is, I want the baby, you don't."

He managed to look even more shocked than he had at his first glance at her, and she couldn't blame him. He was so angry, his blue eyes glinted with icy shards. Deliberately, Kate lifted her chin, met his hard gaze and prepared to do battle.

This baby meant everything to Kate. It was a gift from a universe that had already taken too much from her. She wouldn't lose this child. Wouldn't share it with a man who, if he didn't already, would one day resent its very existence.

"I've talked to you dozens of times over the last five months," he said, his voice quiet, glacial. "Emails. Faxes. Phone calls. *Video* calls. And not *once* did you find the time to say 'By the way, I'm pregnant?'"

Truth was, Kate had been in a kind of fog for the first three months of her pregnancy. At first, she hadn't believed it. Then she'd realized what a miracle had happened. She was finally going to have the family she'd believed lost to her when Sam died. She didn't need a husband, but she needed this baby.

So did Sean.

His heart was pounding, and it felt like he'd taken a hard punch to the gut. He couldn't seem to catch his breath. His gaze was locked on Kate's softly rounded belly as his brain tried to process, think, figure. He hadn't expected this. Sure, he'd known something was up, which was why he'd come to Wyoming the minute Mike and Jenny got back from their honeymoon. But Sean had thought it was a problem with the hotel. Or the crew. *Anything* but this.

They'd used condoms. What was the point of using them if people got pregnant anyway?

Hell, now he knew how Brady Finn had felt when he'd traveled to Ireland to check on the hotel there, only to find that Aine was pregnant. At the time, Sean had taken Aine's side in all of that, telling Brady to get over it and do the right thing. Apparently the universe was getting a kick out of landing him in Brady's exact position.

Scrubbing one hand across his face, Sean fought past the fury choking him and tried to steady himself. The woman who had been haunting him for months was carrying his child. That was fact. That was what he had to focus on now.

But even as he thought it, his past rose up in his mind to remind him that it wasn't the first time he'd found himself in this position. As he fought them, images from ten years before swam to the surface of his mind as if finally released from behind a thick dam.

He'd done a year of college in Italy, and there he'd fallen in love with Adrianna. She was beautiful, smart, funny. And everything was perfect. Until the night she told him she was pregnant. He still felt shame over his reaction, though over the years he'd tried to explain it away by saying he was young. Stupid. Selfish.

But the bottom line was, she had been excited and saw a shiny, happy future for the two of them. All Sean had seen were chains. They had argued viciously and two weeks later, she miscarried the baby she had wanted so badly. Sean went to see her in the hospital, but she turned him away. He could still see her lying on that narrow bed, her beautiful face as white as the sheets beneath her. Her eyes were filled with shadows of pain and a single tear tracked along her cheek.

"Go away," Adrianna had said, turning her face to the wall so she wouldn't have to look at him.

Sean clutched the huge bouquet of roses he'd brought with him and tried again to reach her. To make her see him. To make her realize just how badly he felt. "Adrianna, I'm sorry about the baby."

She spared him a glance then, and in that brief motion he saw that her dark eyes were empty. "You are not sorry, Sean. You didn't want our child. Well, now he is gone so you can be happy. But be happy somewhere else. I don't want you here. I don't want you to come back."

The smell of the hospital, the rumble of nurses and doctors being called over the communication system, the soft moan from an old woman in a bed across the room—none of it mattered. The only thing that mattered was Adrianna, and he was losing her.

His heart breaking, Sean stood his ground, fist tightening on the flowers he held, determined to make her understand why he'd reacted as he had. Make her forgive him. "Adrianna," he whispered, "we can get past this."

"No." She stared at the wall, her fingers clenching on the thin blanket covering her. "No." She took a shuddering breath. "I needed you and you were not there. Now," she added, "I do not need you anymore."

Helpless, Sean had dropped the roses on the chair by the door and left, knowing that he'd lost something precious. That he'd thrown away what some men only dreamed of having.

And he'd lived with the shame and guilt of that for ten years. Never shared it with his brother— with anyone—just carried it around like a lump of ice in a corner of his heart. But now, he had a chance to let go of that past by being the man he should have been when he was too young and self-involved to know better.

Sean looked into Kate's lake-blue eyes and read her determination to keep him out of this. To get him to leave. To walk away from her and his child. But it wasn't going to happen.

He wouldn't fail again.

"You should sit down," he said.

"What?"

"You're pregnant. Sit down." He steered her back to the couch and hovered there until she sat.

"Seriously?" She flipped her long, loose hair back over her shoulder to stare up at him. "I was on the job site today installing new windows and ripping old paneling off walls, and you think it's too strenuous for me to stand in my own living room?"

It sounded stupid when she put it like that. But he was off his game. Hell, knocked off his feet. "So cut me a break. I've known about this baby for like ten seconds. Might take a little longer to get used to it."

"That's my point, Sean. You don't have to get used to it."

"Right." He shoved both hands into his pants pockets. "You really expect that I'll just say 'take care' and walk away?"

The fact that he had done just that ten years ago had nothing to do with this.

"That's my child you're carrying," he snapped, feeling anger and frustration nipping at his insides again, "and it's my responsibility to see to it that it's safe."

"Her."

"What?"

"You said *it*," Kate said tightly. "The baby's a girl."

"A girl." Sean swayed in place as a rush of emotion filled his throat. Another hard hit in a series of them. He had a *daughter*. That knowledge alone made this all the more real. All the more vital. Sean took a breath to steady himself and looked at Kate. Stubborn fury was etched into her features. She was hostile and prepared to dig in her heels to fight him on this.

It fried him that she'd kept this secret. Kept his baby from him and clearly had had no intention of ever telling him about it...*her*. Maybe Kate had her reasons, but at the moment, he didn't give a good damn what they were. So yeah, he remembered telling her that he had no interest in children or a family. And maybe he hadn't really considered it since Italy. He might not have gone out and deliberately tried to be a father, but now that he was faced with the reality of it, he wanted his kid.

He was here and not going anywhere. Kate was going to have to find a way to deal with it. No doubt the two of them would butt heads over this situation, but in the end, Sean would have things his way. Kate had no idea what Sean could do when he was set on a certain path. Hadn't he, his brother and their friend built a billion-dollar business from *nothing*? He hadn't allowed anyone to get in his way then, and he wasn't about to start now. Sean made his living by convincing people that he was right so they would fall into line. Kate would eventually give way, just like everyone else.

First things first, though. "Is the baby all right?"

Her face softened in an instant as she stroked her palm over her belly. "She's fine."

"Good." He nodded and swallowed hard over the sudden knot of lust clogging his throat. Were *all* pregnant women this hot? "That's good."

"Sean," she said on a sigh, "I know what you're doing."

"Is that right?" He tucked his hands into his pockets. "What am I doing, Kate?"

She stood up to face him, and he felt the same surge of desire he had felt the first time he'd met her. Kate Wells affected him as no one else ever had—and pregnancy hadn't changed that a bit. But staring at her now, he wasn't thinking of the baby, or the lies, or the arguments waiting for them in the coming days.

All he saw was the woman who had been in his mind for months. Her eyes were flashing, her mouth was set in a straight, grim line and that stubborn tilt to her chin only made her look more amazing. What the hell did it say about him, he wondered, that he found a woman who looked like she wanted to rip his lips off so damned irresistible?

"You're trying to make me feel badly about not telling you about the baby."

"Don't you?"

She blew out a breath. "Yes, I do. But I did what I thought was best, just like I'm doing now. I want you to leave, Sean."

"We don't always get what we want, Kate."

"How are you even here? How did you find out where I live?" She threw her hands high, then caught herself and paused. "Never mind. Not important. What's important is that you leave. Now."

He grabbed her upper arms and held on to her, when he felt her jerk back in an attempt to free herself. "You weren't that hard to find, Kate. And now that I have found you—and my daughter— I'm not going anywhere."

She paled a little but recovered quickly and went on the defensive. "Sean, you don't have anything to prove. It's nice that you offered to be involved with the baby, but it's not necessary."

"It's not *nice*," he said, feeling that swell of irritation come thick and fast again. "That's my daughter as much as yours, so yeah, me being a part of this *is* necessary. You're not cutting me out, Kate. I'm in this."

Outside, the sun was nearly gone, and Kate reached out to flick on a table lamp. Golden light streamed through the room, and he could see her even more clearly than he had before. She didn't look happy, he thought. Well, that made two of them.

"We've got things to talk about."

"No, Sean, we don't. I'm the one who's pregnant, so I'm the one making decisions." She picked up her teacup, stepped to one side and grabbed Molly's wineglass then headed out of the room, throwing words back over her shoulder. "And since I'm only five months along, I've got plenty of time."

Sean followed right after her. It didn't take long. You could drop her entire living room, dining room and kitchen into the main room of his condo in Long Beach and still have room left over. In the tiny galley-style kitchen, he walked up behind her and, in effect, trapped her there. Backed up against the kitchen sink and hedged between the stove and the refrigerator, all she could do was stare up at him.

"We'll *both* be making any decisions necessary, Kate. I'm not walking away from my kid." He dropped his hands onto the sink's edge on either side of her. "I'm here in Wyoming for the next three days. I'd stay longer, but we've got the release of our latest game next week and I have to be there to help."

"Don't let me stop you," she quipped and ducked beneath his arm to escape him.

But he grabbed her arm and held on. "Oh, you won't. You won't stop me from doing anything." It was a warning and a declaration all at once. It was time she knew that he wasn't going to quietly disappear. She was carrying his baby, and that link bound them together.

She'd just have to get used to it.

# Seven

Kate felt like she was being stalked.

Everywhere she turned, there Sean was. He watched what she ate, what she drank. He hovered over her on the job site until even her crew stopped coming to her with questions and instead spoke to Sean first. She felt the threads of control slipping through her fingers, and there didn't seem to be a thing she could do about it.

When she complained to Sean, he only smiled and shrugged, brushing off her anger as if it didn't bother him a bit. And that only made her more furious.

Molly, of course, was fascinated. While Kate stood beneath a stand of pines at the edge of the lake, she turned her face into the wind and listened to her friend's voice bubbling over the phone.

"I mean, he's even more spectacular in person than he is in all those paparazzi photos." She took a breath and heaved a dramatic sigh. "That's the kind of guy who makes women dissolve into puddles at his feet."

Kate scowled and watched two magpies swoop over the lake to disappear into the trees. "That must be why he keeps expecting me to fall in line."

"Well, why wouldn't you?" Molly asked. "He's gorgeous, rich, you're carrying his baby *and* he wants to be involved." Before Kate could say anything, Molly rushed on. "And let's not forget, you already confessed that the sex was the best you've ever had."

Now Kate winced. She had said that, in spite of feeling disloyal to Sam's memory. Her late husband hadn't been the best lover, but he'd had other, more important qualities that Sean lacked.

Sean was pushy, dictatorial, arrogant—and those were his good points. Okay, yes, he had beautiful eyes and talented hands and a wicked sense of humor that often made Kate laugh even when she didn't want to. But none of that—even including the amazing sex—was enough to build a life on. And he might not have mentioned marriage yet, but he wanted their baby so she was pretty sure he would mention it, sooner or later.

And she would never get married again. Too much opportunity for pain.

"Sex isn't everything," Kate muttered.

A deep voice behind her said, "People who say that aren't doing it right."

Kate inhaled sharply as her heart gave a hard thump. Just hearing his voice set her nerves jangling and her pulse racing—in spite of how hard she tried to rein them in. Blast it, she thought, she'd come out here to get away from Sean for a while. She'd thought she had escaped the hotel cleanly. Hadn't she waited until Sean was in the kitchen with the crew before she slipped out for a little privacy? But no, he'd managed to track her down anyway.

"I heard that," Molly said, laughing. "I'm really starting to like him."

"That makes one of us," Kate muttered. "I've gotta go."

"Fine, but I'll need a full report later. Spare no details."

Kate shook her head and hung up, then turned to face Sean. "Why are you following me?"

He shrugged and the movement stretched his black T-shirt across a chest she had reason to know was a broad expanse of muscle. "Don't think of it as following you. Think of it more like I'm walking my property. Get an idea what the land looks like when it's *not* buried under a hundred feet of snow."

She didn't believe him, even though what he said made sense. Because instead of checking out the scenery, his gaze was fixed on her. Heat blossomed in the center of her chest and sent tendrils of warmth rippling through her. His eyes were as blue as the lake behind her and the wind ruffled his black hair across his forehead. It looked like he hadn't bothered to shave that morning, so a beard shadow covered his jaw and only made him look even sexier—and she wouldn't have thought that possible.

Having him here again, on her turf, was unsettling. When Sean was several hundred miles away, she could focus on her life, her baby, and almost convince herself that Sean wasn't a part of it at all. And that, she told herself, was how she wanted it. What she felt for Sean was a tangle of emotions. The desire was still there, of course, but mixed in was annoyance and an affection she couldn't completely deny.

"Well, take a look around," she said, waving one arm to encompass the wide spill of lake behind them and the forest that ringed the lake and stretched out for miles on either side of the hotel. When his gaze shifted to the view, Kate watched him and softened at his reaction to the beauty around him.

He looked back at her and smiled. "It's a great

spot. Beautiful, really. It's amazing how big the sky looks out here. Seems a lot smaller somehow in California. You know, up until now, I've always been a beach guy. Love surfing, taking a boat out." His gaze shifted back to the calm surface of the sapphire-blue lake that mirrored the white clouds overhead and the pines that stood as guardians at the edge.

She had to smile. "Boats have been known to go on lakes, too."

He grinned, and she felt the jolt of it clutch at her heart.

"Good point," he said. "Maybe we could look into getting some boats here for guests. And paddleboards would probably go over well."

She imagined they would, but said, "Not exactly in line with the theme of ancient warriors and evil creatures."

He laughed easily and tucked his hands into his pockets. "Even gamers take time out for a little reality now and then. And we could paint scenes from the game on them."

Kate sighed. It was so hard to resist when he

poured on that charm. Even knowing she should be hardening her heart, keeping her distance, she was drawn to him like she'd never been drawn to anyone else. And when he smiled at her, as he did now, everything inside her softened, yielded.

He turned to scan the forest area then looked back at Kate. "Why don't you show me where you're going to position the cabins?"

"Okay." Good. This was good. Keep the conversation away from the personal. They were being calm, reasonable and talking about the job. She swallowed down the knot of emotion in her throat and pretended it hadn't been there at all. Reminding herself that he was her boss might be enough to keep her thoughts on the here and now rather than on a distant future that seemed too nebulous to negotiate at the moment.

Pointing to the closest stand of trees, she said, "You can see where we've already laid out the foundation slabs for the first two cabins." She took a few steps and stopped again. "The others complete a half circle around the hotel. While they're tucked into the forest enough to be private, they'll still be close enough to the hotel that guests can easily walk up for the restaurant or gift shops. The septics are in, so that job's done and we'll get started on putting up the cabin frames in the next week or so. Just waiting on the final plans from the architect."

He was walking right beside her, and she swore she could feel heat pumping from his body into hers.

"Sounds good. But why didn't you put a couple of them closer to the lake?"

"Risky," she said. "In a hard winter, the spring runoff could raise the water level, so you don't want to be too close to the edge or you've got flooding worries."

"Good point," he said, shifting his gaze to study the proposed layout of the cabins. "When we get a hard storm surf in Long Beach, people are out sandbagging the sea wall to keep the shore houses from flooding."

Sometimes, it felt as if they were completely in synch. For some reason it seemed that as their personal issues got more complicated, their working relationship improved. Talking about the job, answering questions, making plans, they felt like a team. But that was an illusion. She worked for him, and it was best that she remember that. This was her biggest construction project ever and no matter what else happened between her and Sean, Kate was determined to make the most of this huge opportunity.

"Most of the cabins will have lake views," she said, walking again. The toe of her boot caught on a thick tree root, and she stumbled but caught herself. An instant later, Sean took her elbow to steady her on the uneven forest floor. Heat, raw and undiluted, roared into her body from the simple touch of his hand on her arm. Now she was more unsteady than ever but didn't want to let him know it. "I'm perfectly fine, Sean. I don't need help. I didn't fall."

He shrugged. "Shoot me. My mother raised a gentleman."

"I appreciate it, but I can walk by myself." She tried to pull free, but his grip shifted from velvet to iron in a heartbeat. And being reminded of his strength set up a flutter of nerves in the pit of her stomach.

Sean pulled her around to face him. "Look, I get that you're not used to anyone taking care of you. But you're pregnant with *my* baby now. And I'm going to take care of you—and *her*—whether you like it or not."

And there went the closeness, the sensation of teamwork. He couldn't seem to help himself from that arrogant, I-know-best attitude.

"You can't just show up out of nowhere and start throwing your weight around," Kate told him. "*You* are not in charge."

"Wrong." The word snapped from him and the heat in his eyes flashed dangerously. "From here on out, Kate, I'm giving the orders."

"Are you serious?" She matched his fury with that of her own. "I've been on my own for a long time now. I don't need you, Sean."

Something dark and pain-filled flashed briefly in his eyes but was gone again in seconds. "Need me or not, I'm here, and you're not shaking me loose so get used to it."

They glared at each other, neither of them willing to back down. All around them, the wind whispered in the trees, birds shrieked and in the lake, a fish shot from the water to dive back in with a soft splash.

Then Sean muttered, "Damn it, what is it about you anyway?"

He dragged her in tight and kissed her hard. She thought about resisting on principle, but she couldn't hold out against him. Her mouth softened against his as her blood pumped fast and thick in her veins. God, she'd missed this. The rising need, the tingles of anticipation and excitement that were bubbling through her. She held on to him, loving the feel of his strong arms wrapping around her, holding her close.

It was crazy, and all too quickly it was over.

When she opened her eyes, Kate saw Sean staring down at her and smug satisfaction shining in his eyes. "Don't need me, huh?"

Like ice water had been dumped on her head, coldness swamped her, putting out the fire she'd felt only seconds before.

"You kiss me then throw my reaction in my face?" Kate was practically vibrating with frustration and a simmering anger that burned so brightly she was surprised her skin wasn't glowing with it.

"Just reminding you of what's between us," he said tightly, and she had some satisfaction knowing that the kiss had affected him just as it had her.

"I know exactly what's between us," Kate said and slapped one hand to her belly.

He covered her hand with his. "Now I do, too. And I promise you, I'm not going anywhere."

"Am I interrupting something?"

At the sound of the deep voice, both of them turned to face the older man approaching.

"Dad?" Kate looked at her father in surprise. She'd been so caught up in Sean, she hadn't heard anything beyond the thundering beat of her own heart. "What're you doing here?"

Harry Baker was a tall man, with steel-gray hair, piercing blue eyes, a barrel chest and heavily muscled arms from years of working construction. Normally easygoing and friendly, at the moment Harry's features were tight and grim.

"Raul called," he said, answering Kate while keeping his gaze on Sean. "Asked me to come help him install the new windows on the third floor."

Kate nearly groaned. She'd forgotten that her father would be on the job site today. Frankly, with Sean around, it was hard to concentrate on anything else. If she'd remembered, she could have prepared Sean. Heck, prepared *herself* for a confrontation that had been building for months.

She took a breath to steady herself. Her father had been after her for months to tell Sean the truth and to stop working. Ever since her mother had died, when Kate was twelve, Harry had been everything to Kate. He'd raised her, taught her, loved her and worried about her. Having her pregnant and unmarried chipped at something inside him, and Kate knew it had taken every ounce of his self-control not to call Sean himself and tell him what was going on.

"That's right. I forgot." There was too much

going on, she told herself. But with most of the crew busy finishing off the main kitchen and digging out the basement to make room for the large utility ramp they'd be installing, Raul did need the help.

Her father was glaring at Sean, and she knew he'd come looking for them deliberately so he could have a talk with the man who'd impregnated his daughter. God, she felt as though she was living in a nineteenth century romance. The men in her life were suddenly becoming cavemen, and there were definite signs of testosterone poisoning.

"Well, Dad," she said, keeping her voice light and a smile on her face, "this is Sean Ryan."

"I guessed as much." He didn't smile in return.

Sean offered his hand. "Good to meet you."

Kate watched as the two men took each other's measure during the space of a handshake that looked more like a contest of wills than a polite greeting. This was so not a female moment.

As if agreeing with her, Sean said tightly, "Kate, why don't you go on back to the hotel while your dad and I have a talk?"

Exactly what she'd been planning to do until Sean suggested it. "Stop telling me what to do."

"Kate, go away."

She looked at her father. "You, too, Dad?"

Neither of the men was looking at her, and that only infuriated her well beyond what little patience she had left. She might as well be at the hotel. These two had already dismissed her. "Fine. I'm going back to work."

"Be careful," Sean warned.

"For heaven's sake…" Her mutter carried even while she walked away.

Sean spared her a single glance, then turned his focus back to the man staring at him. Awkward, he told himself, but no getting around it.

"I didn't know she was pregnant," Sean said, once Kate was out of earshot.

"I know." Harry's eyes were narrowed on him. "I disagreed with her on that, wanted her to tell you, but she's a strong woman. Hardheaded, too."

"Yeah, I know," Sean said. "I like that about her."

Harry snorted and relaxed his stance enough

that Sean was pretty sure he wasn't about to be punched. Funny how facing down the father of the woman you're sleeping with could make a man feel like a teenager caught breaking curfew.

"Kate's a grown woman and her decisions are her own, no matter how I'd like to think different."

Sean thought he could see the man's point of view and now that he knew he was also going to be the father of a daughter, he had to wonder if he'd be as reasonable as Harry Baker was in the same situation. Of course, Sean's daughter would never be in this situation because he was never going to let a man near his girl. But for now, he had to reassure Kate's father.

"She's not alone in this," Sean told the other man quietly. "Now that I know about the baby, I'm in this and she's not going to shake me loose."

Harry tipped his head to one side and studied Sean. His eyes were sharp, and Sean thought he probably didn't miss much. Made him uncomfortable having that steady gaze fixed on him, but he stood his ground and waited.

"Good to know," Harry said with a nod. "But I'm thinking it's my daughter that brought you here."

Sean frowned. He had come to see Kate. To see if he had imagined the connection between them—which he hadn't. Hell, his mouth was still burning, his body still sizzling just from that one short, furious kiss they'd shared. He didn't know what the hell was between him and Kate, but he did know they had to figure it out before he talked to her father about all of this.

Instead, he said only, "It's my hotel, Mr. Baker. I've got to keep an eye on the progress."

Shaking his head, Harry mused, "You check out every hotel with a kiss?"

Sean scowled and rubbed one hand across the back of his neck. "Yeah, you saw that."

"I did. Look, what's between you is private." Harry folded beefy arms across his wide chest and stood like a man braced for a fight. "But I'll say I want my pregnant daughter married."

*Married?* Amazing how that one small word could hit a man like a bucket of rocks. Nobody had said anything about getting married, Sean thought. He could understand how Harry felt, but marriage was something that seemed so… forever. *But so*, his mind whispered, *is a baby.* A child. Linking him and Kate always.

Hell, he hadn't had enough time to think things through. To make a plan. To figure out what his response should be. There was too much going on in his head right now to make sense of much of it. But he did know he wanted his kid. He wanted the chance to prove—if only to himself—that he wasn't the same man he once was. That he'd grown and changed.

Harry was still talking, though, so Sean listened.

"This is the first real sign of life I've seen in my girl since she lost her husband."

*"Husband?"*

Harry's eyebrows lifted. "Didn't know about Sam, eh? Well, not surprising. My girl isn't what you'd call a big sharer." He frowned to himself. "Losing Sam threw her hard. She doesn't really talk about it, but I can see it. She changed after

Sam. Locked herself down." He paused and gave Sean another long look. "Until you, that is."

Sean didn't know what to say to that. She'd never mentioned being married. Being widowed. Why the news hit him so hard was beyond him. But just knowing she'd once been another man's wife was hard to deal with. What was he like, the mystery husband? As he wondered, he remembered their conversation last winter and how she'd only been with one other man.

He groaned internally. Hell, no wonder she'd been so defensive of a man who hadn't been much of a lover. He'd been her *husband*. She'd loved the guy and clearly remained loyal to him even now. There was a tightness in Sean's chest he didn't care for, so he rubbed his fist against his breastbone in a futile effort to ease the discomfort. Weird position to be in, he thought as he recognized what he was feeling. Envious of a dead man.

"She and Sam talked about having a family, but then he was gone and Kate sort of…" Harry paused then said, "Shut down. Like she pulled away from life because it was just too painful. But since you, and now the baby, she's been different. More like herself than I've seen in a while."

Was she still in love with the long-gone Sam? Sean didn't much care for that thought and didn't care to explore why the idea bothered him as much as it did. He had his own past, didn't he? He hadn't told her about Adrianna and the baby. Hadn't opened up his soul.

Passion had brought them together, and Fate had thrown them both a curve by creating a child to mark the occasion.

What the hell was he supposed to do with this information?

He was going home in a couple of days. He had to be in California for the launch of "The Wild Hunt." But how could he leave Kate and his child behind?

"Are you crazy?" Kate demanded a few hours later. "I can't go to California. We're in the middle of a job!"

Sean folded his arms across his chest and leaned one shoulder against the doorjamb. His eyes were cool, almost amused, and that just fed the outrage rushing through her. Sean and her father had walked in from their forest meeting like old friends, each of them smiling, until they caught sight of her. Then the two of them had presented a united front of keeping her in the dark.

Had they cooked this up between them?

"I told you that you couldn't march into my life and start issuing orders," she reminded him. "And if you and my dad think you can make plans for me like I'm a child who needs two strong men to take care of me, then you're both crazy."

Casually, he crossed one foot over the other and looked, she thought, not just amused, but *bored* by her arguments. "This has nothing to do with your father. I have to be back at the office to help run the launch of the new game—"

"So, go," she told him quickly, both relieved and somehow disappointed to know he was leaving. But she'd get over it. "Happy trails."

He snorted and shook his head as he watched her. She wished for an interruption. But that wasn't going to happen.

They were alone in the hotel, with the crew and her father having left more than a half hour ago. Kate had lingered behind to make sure everything was safely tucked away for the night. Tools, extension cords, coffeepots, radios. She'd checked every window on the ground floor and every door lock. They were far enough out in the country that they probably didn't have to worry about thieves or vandals dropping by, but it didn't hurt to make sure things were safe.

Naturally, Sean had stayed, too. As he'd promised earlier, she'd been unable to shake him loose. Now she knew why. He'd waited until they were alone to spring his ridiculous idea.

Outside, the light was going soft and pearly as the sky deepened toward the coming night. Inside, there were only a few lights on, keeping the shadows at bay.

"Oh, I'm going, and you're coming with me."

He looked so sure of himself, Kate wanted to kick him. "The job—"

"Is at a stage where you can leave your crew working without supervision for a few days."

"Days?"

"Maybe a week." He shrugged as if unconcerned about the time he was demanding she take.

"It's business, Kate." Before she could argue again, he said, "I want you out there to meet with our artists. They've had some ideas on the new cabins, and you can consult with them and meet with the architect in person."

"It's not necessary," she argued, already feeling as if she'd lost this battle. He looked calm and in control, and she felt the ragged threads of *her* control sliding from her fingers, but she made one more try. "As long as I have the plans, we'll get it done."

Sean sighed and shook his head. "You're going to lose this one, Kate. This is my job, and I want my contractor in California for a meeting."

He was right. She couldn't win here. He was

not only the man currently driving her insane, but he was also her boss. Refusing to go with him just wasn't an option. But whatever he said, this wasn't only about business. He had an ulterior motive. She just wasn't sure what it was. To get her out of her comfort zone? To *show* her the difference in their lifestyles? To prove that if he wanted their baby, he had the money and power to take it?

Anxiety rippled in the pit of her stomach, and she had the distinct feeling it wouldn't be dissipating anytime soon.

"Pack for a week," he said casually, then glanced around the great room as if the subject was closed. "You were right about these floors," he mused. "Sanded and refinished they look brand-new and old at the same time."

Automatically, her gaze dropped to the floorboards. In the dim light, they shone golden, with a soft gleam that caught the light and held it. Yes, the hotel was looking good. Walls were painted, floors refinished, ceiling beams stripped and sanded until they looked as they had when the place was first built. But at the moment, she didn't feel like admiring her crew's work.

"Yeah, oak will do that. But back to the point—"

"The point is," he interrupted her neatly, "we leave day after tomorrow. Be ready."

# Eight

It started with a private jet.

The minute she walked on board, Kate knew that she would never be happy flying coach again. There were luxurious leather seats, plush carpeting so thick her shoes sank in it and a flight attendant whose sole duty was to ensure that Kate enjoyed the trip to California. Sadly, the very efficient woman couldn't ease the knot of nerves in Kate's stomach.

That knot only tightened once they landed, and Sean drove them to his penthouse condo on the beach. Stepping into that expansive space was a revelation. Sean gave the impression of being a regular guy who liked surfing. She had known, of course, just how rich he was, but his home really defined the difference between her life and his.

The living room was wide and furnished with tasteful comfort in mind. Polished wood floors were dotted with thick rugs in neutral tones.´ Couches and chairs were overstuffed, inviting visitors to drop down and be comfortable. A wall of windows provided an amazing view of the Pacific, and with the French doors opened to a terrace that stretched the length of the building, a sea breeze drifted lazily into the room.

Anxious, Kate wandered through the condo and let the silence inside her, where hopefully it would settle the nerves clawing at her. She was alone now, as she had been the night before, sleeping in one of the guest rooms in this palace. Sean hadn't pushed for her to join him in his bed, and a part of her had been disappointed in that.

This morning when she woke, Sean was already gone. But he'd left her a note in the living room.

Went surfing. Make yourself at home. I'll be back in a couple hours and we'll go to the office.

So Kate made coffee in the incredible kitchen and tried not be envious of the six-burner stove, the sub-zero fridge and the miles of black granite. She was willing to bet the man never cooked anything more than a cup of coffee and maybe toast. No way he could really appreciate this kitchen for the incredible work space it was.

Sighing, she took her coffee onto the terrace and sat down on one of the cushioned chairs arranged there to enjoy the view. In June, gray skies covered the coast of California every morning, keeping the heat down and giving the Pacific a leaden look. The ocean was immense and frothed with white caps. Boats, their brightly colored sails billowing in the wind, skimmed across the surface of the water, and near the shore she could make out a handful of surfers riding the waves.

"Is one of them Sean?" Kate watched, thought about the man who'd brought her here and wondered what the hell she was going to do for the next few days.

Having him on her turf was hard enough, but being on *his,* completely pulled her out of her comfort zone… She kept losing her mental balance and wasn't sure how to get it back—or even if she would.

When her phone rang, she answered gratefully. "Molly, hi."

"Hi, yourself. How's it going?"

"Well, I'm sitting here on the private terrace of a truly awesome penthouse, staring out at the ocean."

"Wow," Molly said on a sigh. "Sounds rough."

Kate laughed shortly. Trust Molly to put things in perspective. "Okay, his home is beautiful and looks like a spread in a magazine. You should see the kitchen."

"Uh-huh, unlike you, I really don't care about kitchen goodies. What about Sean? What's happening with you two?"

"Nothing." Kate sipped at her coffee and sighed. "I don't know why I'm here. I swear, even though he insisted this trip was about business, there was a part of me that figured he was just trying to get me out here and into his bed." Well, boy, *that* sounded egotistical. "You know, keep me happy long enough that he could find a way to get our baby."

"Come on, Kate…"

"But he didn't try anything last night." Frustration jumped into life and held hands with the anxiety inside her. "Nothing. He just showed me the guest room."

And that fact, she was forced to admit, had bothered her more than a little. She'd lain awake half the night, imagining him in the room across the hall and wishing that she was lying next to him, which made her…what? Pitiful? Crazy? Masochistic?

"Well," Molly sympathized, "that's just sad."

"It really *is*. But more than sad," Kate told her, "it's out of character. He's been flirting with me and trying to seduce me since we met. Now all of a sudden, nothing? He's been really quiet, too, and that's really not like him. Plus, I keep finding him watching me."

"That doesn't sound like a bad thing."

"Not *that* kind of watching. This is more studying, like I was a bug under a microscope and he's trying to figure out exactly what species I am."

"You're overreacting, honey," Molly said, and Kate could almost *see* her shaking her head slowly.

But Molly didn't know Sean like Kate did. Okay, they hadn't known each other for very long, but their relationship had been pretty intense right from the beginning. Being with Sean made Kate feel more alive than she did without him. She liked arguing with him, liked laughing with him and she loved being held by him. *Loved?*

That word sneaked in there unexpectedly and for the moment, Kate was going to ignore it.

"I think he's up to something."

"Paranoid much?" Molly asked, laughing.

"Molly, he told me he wants the baby." She looked over her shoulder into the living room of the condo. "Judging by this place, the private jet, if he wanted to, he could go for custody and I wouldn't stand a chance."

Instantly her friend's attitude shifted. "Don't do this to yourself, Kate. Don't go looking for trouble. Wait for it to find you if it's coming."

"Hard to be prepared if you're waiting," Kate said, shifting her gaze back to the cool, blue ocean. On the other hand there was just no preparing for Sean Ryan. He was like a force of nature, blowing into her life and turning it all upside down.

"Kate, do yourself a favor," Molly said softly. "Just enjoy where you are while you're there. Stop worrying about what might happen before it does."

Good advice, Kate thought a few minutes later when she hung up. She just didn't know if she could follow it or not. Worry was simply a part of who she was. As a kid, after her mother's death, she'd worried that her father would die, too. She'd insisted on going with him to job sites whenever she wasn't in school, just to keep an eye on him. Later, she'd worried about classes and worried when she married Sam that something would go wrong to ruin their happiness.

That time, she'd been right.

So how could she stop worrying about the possibility of losing her child?

"Kate? You here?"

She stood up and turned to see Sean striding into the condo. For one split second, she did exactly as Molly had advised and simply enjoyed the view. His hair was still damp, his jaw shadowed with whiskers. He had a cherry-red surfboard tucked under his left arm and the wetsuit he wore had been pulled down to his waist, leaving his arms and chest bare.

Heat erupted so fast, so completely, it stole her breath. Kate dragged in a gulp of air and forced herself to lift her gaze from his chest to meet his eyes. Once she did, she saw a flash of recognition shining there, and she knew that he was aware of what she'd been feeling.

But how could he be, she wondered, when she'd just that second realized she was in love with him?

She swayed a little as the knowledge settled

into her brain to stay. Kate had been fighting her own emotions for too long. She had tried to ignore them, pretend that all she felt for Sean was the closeness associated with a lover—and the father of her child. She'd even tried to ignore the feelings altogether and when that didn't work, she'd lied to herself about the truth that was even now slamming home.

She couldn't be in love with a man in the position to take everything she cared about away from her. Couldn't give him even more power over her than he already had. Panic settled into the pit of her stomach, and she swallowed hard. After Sam, she'd vowed to never love again. To never put herself in a position to experience the pain of loss again. But it seemed that life happened even when you tried to avoid it.

"Hey!" Sean dropped the surfboard with a clatter and crossed to her in a blink. Holding on to her arms and looking into her eyes, he asked, "Are you okay? Your face just went snow-white. Is it the baby?"

He smelled so good was all she could think.

But she managed to tie a rope around a single active brain cell, then dragged it around until it collected enough friends that she could speak again.

"I'm fine." His eyes shone with worry. "Really. I'm fine. So's the baby." She changed the subject quickly before he could grab her and rush her off to a doctor or something. "Did you have a good time?"

"Waves weren't much, but it was good to be out there again." He shrugged, then reached up and ran both hands through his hair. His muscled chest rippled until Kate wanted nothing more than to stroke her palms across it. Deliberately, she curled her hands into fists.

"I'm going to grab a fast shower," Sean said into the silence. "Then we'll head over to the office."

"Okay." She didn't want to think about him in the shower and wondered if he'd planted that image in her brain on purpose. But the way he walked out of the room, easily dismissing her, sort of shot down that theory.

So what was he up to? What was his plan?

* * *

Sean didn't have a plan.

He was still thinking about the fact that Kate had been someone's *wife* and hadn't told him. What the hell was that about? He'd seen the look in her eye this morning when he got home from the beach. Passion. Desire. Need. It was all there, easily enough read in spite of her attempts to hide it. But damn if he'd be a substitute for her dead husband. It had taken every ounce of self-control he had to keep from stalking across the room and grabbing her. Then she'd gone so white, anger had been swamped by a flood of panic.

He was keeping an eye on her to make sure she didn't do that again. And once Sean was sure she was okay, he would need some answers.

He watched her working with the art department and heard the deep, rich music of her laughter at something Dave said. She flipped her long, loose hair back and bent over Dave's shoulder as he made notations on a computer.

"Does she have to get *that* close?" he muttered.

"I like her."

Sean shot his brother a sour look, not pleased that he'd been so focused on Kate that Mike had been able to sneak up on him.

"Yeah, she's good. Did you see how quickly she picked up on the ideas for different rooflines on the cabins? I liked how she tweaked them, too, so each cabin will have a different look and style."

"I noticed," Mike said, giving his brother a shoulder bump, "but I wasn't talking about her work. I like *her*. She's nice. Funny. Pretty, too."

Sean rolled his eyes. Mike wasn't exactly subtle. "She is. Kate and Jenny seem to have hit it off."

Mike nodded and watched his wife join Kate and Dave at the computer. All three of them were talking over each other to the point where Sean had to wonder how they could get anything done. His gaze fixed on Kate, in her black slacks and the tight, short-sleeved yellow shirt that defined and displayed her rounded belly. Something inside him stirred, a sense of protectiveness, possession, that surprised him with its depth. And there was something else there, as well. It wasn't just the baby he wanted, it was Kate.

"You're staring," Mike murmured.

"What?" Sean shot him a quick look. "The only way you would know that is because you're watching *me*. Cut it out. Don't you have somewhere to be?"

"Nope, the beauty of being a boss. I can be wherever I want to be. And right now, I want to watch my brother drool over a pregnant woman." Mike grinned when Sean turned his head to stare at him. "Something you'd like to tell the class?"

Sean jerked his head then walked off, knowing his brother would follow. Once in Mike's office with the door closed, Sean paced, hands in his pockets, too restless to stand still.

"So? It's your baby, isn't it?"

Sean stopped, took a breath and looked at Mike. "Yeah, it is. *She* is."

"A daughter?" Mike grinned widely. "That's excellent. Congratulations. We find out our baby's sex tomorrow."

Sean nodded, knowing just how excited Mike

was about the baby Jenny was carrying. They'd made a family, they were building a future. Right now, all Sean had was the knowledge that he would be a father. He'd never really been one to look into the future. He was more of a right-now kind of guy. But a lot was changing in his life lately.

"That's great, Mike," he said, dragging one hand through his hair. "Really."

"Yeah, it is." Mike walked across the room and sat on the edge of his desk. "What's going on, Sean?"

"Oh," he said, snorting a laugh, "not much. I just found out I'm going to be a father. The woman carrying my kid wants nothing to do with me, and did I mention she used to be married but her sainted husband died two years ago?"

"Whoa. That's a lot."

"You think?" Sean dropped into a chair, stretched his legs out in front of him and folded his hands on his abdomen. "It bugs the hell out of me that she didn't tell me she was married before." He shook his head. "I mean, sure we haven't known each other long and she really didn't have a reason to tell me, but why didn't she? Hell, I don't even know *why* it bugs me so much."

"Don't you?" Mike asked.

"Is she still in love with the dead guy, Mike?"

"I don't know," his brother said thoughtfully. "Why don't you ask her?"

"Because she should have told me about Saint Sam," he snapped. This had been gnawing on his gut since Kate's dad told him about her marriage and how it had ended. He'd been biting his tongue for days to keep from saying something because damn it he wanted *her* to tell him. But it was looking like that wasn't going to happen, so he'd have to do something to end this. Did she kiss *him* and think of Sam? Because Sean wasn't going to stand for that.

"Look," Mike said, "you gave me some good advice not long ago when Jenny was making me crazy—"

"Not the same thing," Sean said, cutting off his

brother. Mike had been in love with Jenny. Sean was in lust with Kate. *Big* difference.

"Right." Mike shook his head impatiently. "Anyway, the point is, you told me I should talk to her, get everything out, and you were right. Why don't you take your own advice? Talk to her, Sean. For God's sake, you're having a baby together. Maybe you should work some of this stuff out?"

"Yeah. The question is, how?" Sean jumped from the chair and prowled the office again, as if he was trapped and looking for a way out. Throwing a look at Mike, he said, "I don't have time for this right now. We've got the big launch next week, and there's a million details to refine yet."

"Uh-huh."

"We're still putting together the storyboards for 'Dragon's Tears'—and that comes out in December, we've got to get those finalized..."

"Uh-huh."

Sean stopped dead and fired a look at his

brother. "Just say what you're thinking. You agreeing with me so easily is a little creepy."

"Fine." Mike came off the desk and faced him. "We've always got a launch or a new game in the pipe and hopefully, it'll be like that for the next fifty years. But you get to have a life, too, Sean, and sometimes you have to make the time for it."

He scrubbed one hand across the back of his neck. "Make time."

"Yeah. You brought Kate out here—take advantage of having her on your home court, so to speak. Figure out what the hell it is you want, then go and get it and stop giving me a headache."

Sean laughed and shook his head. Leave it to family to wrap things up so neatly. "Wow. Touching. Okay, fine. Speaking of taking some time, I won't be in tomorrow."

"Good. Improve your attitude before you do come back, okay?"

"Gonna work on that," Sean said and left.

Several hours later, Kate was sitting across the table from Sean in the most elegant restaurant she'd ever seen. Candlelight flickered on every table, white linen cloths were brightened by deep red napkins and the sparkle and shine of crystal and silver. Quiet conversations sifted through the room and soft, classical music was a whispered backdrop.

Kate smoothed her napkin across the lap of her new black dress and looked at the gorgeous man opposite her. In jeans and a work shirt, Sean was hard to resist. In a well-tailored black suit with a sapphire-blue tie, he was amazing. He looked as if he'd been born to be in places like this. Actually, he was as comfortable in this rarified atmosphere as Kate was uneasy. Just one more reason that loving him was going to bring nothing but trouble.

"You look beautiful," he said, shattering her thoughts.

"Thank you." She'd had to go shopping, of course, since she hadn't brought anything with her that would have been good enough for a place like this.

There'd been a tension between them all day.

Well, Kate admitted silently, Sean had been… different, since they'd left Wyoming. For her, realizing she was in love made her cautious, afraid she might somehow let the truth slip and set herself up for pain. So the two of them did a careful dance, where every word was weighed and measured and what *wasn't* said lay between them like a minefield.

Conversation during dinner had been stilted, and Kate felt as though she was balancing on a tightrope, trying desperately not to fall.

"How do you like California so far?"

She smiled at him. "What I've seen is beautiful. I love the view from your terrace."

He nodded, and one corner of his mouth tipped up. "That's the reason I bought it. I like seeing the ocean when I wake up."

"You can see it from your bedroom?"

One eyebrow lifted. "If you'd joined me last night, you could have found out for yourself this morning."

"You didn't invite me."

"You don't need an invitation and you know it."

Oh, if she had joined him last night, the view would have been the last thing she was interested in. Even as her body stirred, she let that go and said instead, "This is actually my second trip to California. Of course, on the first trip I was ten and my parents took me to Disneyland."

He smiled, and this time the smile reached his eyes. "Every kid should get the chance to go there."

"You probably went all the time, growing up here."

"Not really. My folks were more about going camping and exploring rather than amusement parks."

"Tonight, you don't look like a camping kind of guy."

"And you don't look much like a contractor who wears a tool belt like other women wear diamonds."

"But that is who I am." Waving one hand to encompass the restaurant, she said, "Places like this, not really a part of my life."

"They could be," he mused.

"Not a lot of five-star restaurants in a little town in Wyoming." Her heartbeat sped up, but before it could get out of hand, Kate reined it in. Her life wasn't here in California. Even if by some miracle she and Sean could find a way to make things work between them, she still couldn't stay here. She had a business, people depending on her, and besides, she wanted to raise her child where she'd grown up.

In a place with more trees than people. Summer nights of lying on a blanket in the yard watching the stars. Fourth of July town picnics, snowmen and ice skating on the lake. Small schools and big dreams. She wanted that for her child and knew she wouldn't be able to find it here in California.

His fingers tapped lightly against the table as he studied her.

"You're staring at me again," she said.

"I like the view," he said, taking a sip of his coffee.

"You're doing the charming thing again," Kate said and smiled a little. "I wondered if I'd see it again."

"What's that mean?"

"Just that I've never seen you as quiet as you have been the last two days."

His gaze dropped deliberately to her belly. "A lot to think about lately."

"You're right about that." She shifted a little under his steady stare. So much to say, she thought, and no way to say it. She changed the subject to one less personal, one less fraught with emotions neither of them was willing to discuss. "So do you come here often for business dinners?"

He smiled and in the candlelight, his eyes glittered. "Not really."

"But you brought me here." She tipped her head to one side. "Why?"

"You didn't enjoy your dinner?"

"It was wonderful, but that doesn't answer my question."

"Easy answer, then. I wanted to take you someplace nice." He stood up, came around to her side and helped her to her feet. "Now, I want to show you something else."

She slipped her hand into his and felt the sizzle of electricity that always happened when he touched her. How would she live without feeling that every day? Would she spend the rest of her life wondering what he was doing? Missing him?

Rising, she looked up into his eyes and asked, "Where are we going?"

His mouth curved briefly. "It's a secret. You like secrets, don't you, Kate?"

They drove down the coast and in his Porsche, the miles flew by. On her right, the ocean shone and sparkled in moonlight that danced on its inky surface. On her left was the man who had so thoroughly breached what she had believed to be well-honed defenses. His charm and his smile had attracted her and now his quiet distance drew her in even further. Was it the baby that had changed him so completely? Was he thinking about how to gain custody? Was he regretting saying he wanted their child?

And what had he meant when he said she liked secrets?

She glanced at him as he steered the sleek car

down the crowded road that ran alongside the beach. Why was he suddenly so hard to read? When they'd first met, she'd dismissed him as an arrogant rich man—now she knew he was much more than that. But what was driving him now?

"Now who's staring?" he asked.

"Just trying to figure you out."

He laughed and it was a short, sharp sound. "I'm not that deep, Kate. You don't have to try so hard."

"I wouldn't have to try at all if you'd just tell me what's going on."

"No fun not knowing what's going on, is it?"

She bit her bottom lip to keep from responding. She knew he was making a crack about her not telling him about the baby. But she'd done what she thought was right, and that was all anyone could do. Besides, she'd apologized for that, hadn't she?

She didn't say another word as he steered the car into a right turn by a sign announcing View Point. He parked, got out of the car then came around and helped her out, as well. Tucking her hand in his, he pulled her along behind him as he walked to the short, white barrier that stood at the edge of the cliff.

Theirs was the only car in the narrow lot, and the roar from the cars on the road seemed muffled somehow beneath the sigh of the ocean below. A sharp, cold wind plucked at the hem of her dress, and the three-inch heels she wore weren't made for crossing uneven asphalt at the pace needed to keep up with Sean's long legs. But finally, he drew her to a stop beside him, with the really insufficient white fence the only thing between them and the long drop to the rocks below.

"This is one of my favorite spots," Sean said, pitching his voice to carry over the wind, the sea and the highway behind them. "Used to come here when I got my first car. I'd sit on the hood and watch the sea for hours."

"It's beautiful," she said. And only a little unnerving to be so close to the edge of a cliff.

"Yeah, it is." He pointed, and her gaze tracked in that direction. "When it's clear like this, you can see all the way up the coast. Sometimes you can see Catalina, too. On a foggy night, it looks like something from out of a dream. Most nights, though, are like tonight and from up here, the beach city lights don't look too bright, too harsh, too crowded."

Listening to him, Kate could see him as a teenager, out here in the dark, alone, watching the world. Hadn't she done the same thing when she would go to the lake as a kid and watch the moon and stars dance over the surface of the water?

"It's a lot more lights than I'm used to seeing at night."

"You have lights, too," he said, with a half smile. "They're called stars. I've never seen so many, and I've been camping in the desert."

"It's true." She looked up and saw maybe a quarter of the stars she would have seen at home. There were just too many lights here to let the sky shine as it should.

She shivered in the wind and shifted her gaze to the bottom of the cliff, where waves slapped hard against the rocks and sent frothy spray into the air.

"Cold?"

"A little." A lot actually, but when he dropped his arm around her shoulders and pulled her in tightly to him, cold was just a memory.

"When I was a kid," he said, "I'd come here, and no one would know where I was. This place was my secret."

There was that word again, Kate thought, looking up at him to find his gaze fixed on hers. "You keep talking about secrets. What is it, Sean?"

His eyes narrowed against the wind as he stared at her. After a few seconds, Kate thought he was going to ignore her question. Then he asked, "Why didn't you tell me you were married? That your husband died?"

# Nine

Kate felt all the air whoosh out of her lungs, and it took her a second or two to refill them. His arm around her tightened in response to her instinctive push to back away from him. *Her father.* Kate closed her eyes briefly when she realized her dad must have told Sean about Sam.

She should have expected it. Anticipated it. Harry Baker was *not* happy that his pregnant daughter was unmarried. She probably should have been grateful that he hadn't come after Sean with a shotgun. Instead, he'd done what he could to convince the father of his grandchild to do what Harry would think was the "right thing."

Now, Sean's arm around her felt like a cage, keeping her where she didn't want to be. She needed a little space, a little breathing room. "Let me go."

"No. Talk to me."

"About what?" She shook her hair back from her face when the wind tossed it across her eyes. "Sounds like my dad already told you everything."

"Not everything," Sean argued, turning her in his arms until she was facing him, pressed up against him. "He couldn't tell me why you kept Sam a secret from me."

She looked everywhere but into his eyes. How could she have told him about her late husband? "Because my marriage had nothing to do with what happened between us."

"That's what you think?" He took her chin and tilted up her face until she had no choice but to meet his gaze. Kate didn't like the shine of anger there, but she was surprised by the layer of hurt she saw over it.

"Okay, when was I supposed to tell you, Sean? *Before* sex or directly after?"

"It wasn't just sex, Kate." His grip on her tightened. "What happened between us was more than that, and you should have told me. God knows there was plenty of time when we were snowbound."

Yeah, he was angry. But instead of convincing her to back down, his anger served to kindle her own. "Just how was I supposed to work that information in, Sean? I know, 'Help me pull out the carpet upstairs and oh, by the way, did I mention I'm a widow?'" She set both hands on his chest and gave a shove. "Let me go, damn it."

He did, and Kate stalked off a few steps before she turned around to face him again. He hadn't moved. Just stood there, a tall presence whose features now looked as if they'd been carved in stone.

"I don't talk about Sam," she blurted out. "Not

to anyone. He's gone, that's all, and when he died, a piece of me died with him."

"Kate…"

"No," she snapped, holding one hand up to get him to be quiet. She'd done this. Opened herself up to this. Memories of Sam tangled with new ones of times with Sean and twisted her up into knots of pain and regret.

Damn it, why did she have to love him? Losing Sam had hurt so badly, and she knew that losing Sean was going to be worse—not only because what she felt for him went deeper than what she'd known with Sam. But because she would also be losing him and still have to live knowing that he was alive and well—just not with her.

So she struggled against the misery curled in her heart and said, "You wanted to hear it, so just be quiet and listen." She had to take a deep breath and steel herself against the flood of memories that swept through her. "We were happy," she finally said. "Sam was a sweet man with a kind smile and a big heart. We were married a couple of years, talking about starting a family.

Then there was an accident on a job site and he was killed.

"He's been gone two years now. And when he died, my dream of kids, a family of my own, went with him."

Sean's eyes narrowed, and a muscle in his jaw twitched as he ground his teeth together. She felt the power of his stare slamming into her, heard the rawness of his voice when he said flatly, "Until you found out you were pregnant."

"Yes." She curled her arms protectively across her belly. "This baby is a miracle for me, Sean. Dreams I let die are alive again because of her."

"That's why you didn't tell me," Sean said, taking two long strides that brought him right up in front of her. "As long as you didn't tell me about my kid, you could pretend that it was Sam's."

Kate's head jerked back as if she'd been slapped. Her throat filled, and her stomach churned. She fought for air and thanked God for the sharp, cold wind that batted the tears from her eyes before they could fall. Staring up into the face of the man she thought she knew and seeing none of the warm humor and charm she was so used to, Kate could only think...*he's right*.

She had done that. And now she was caught with the truth and what it had done to Sean. She had played mental games with herself. Pretended that the baby she carried was the child she and Sam had wanted so badly, because she hadn't wanted to involve Sean at all. What they'd shared had been so momentary—how could she call him later and say she was pregnant and expect anything from him?

*But it hadn't been momentary at all*, her mind whispered, and that's what had really scared her.

Those snowbound days with Sean had opened up her heart, her mind, her soul. He'd touched places inside her that no one else ever had, and it had scared her. Scared her enough that she'd found a way to avoid seeing him again. And now, being called on it, she could understand Sean's anger and the hurt she'd caught such a brief glimpse of.

She wanted to argue with him, tell him he was

wrong, but she couldn't. The truth was hard, but lying wouldn't solve anything at this point.

"God." Shaking her head, she said, "You're right, Sean. I did try to pretend that this was Sam's baby. We wanted a family, and I felt cheated when Sam died." She threw up her hands. "We had a few days together, you and I, and what we felt and did was so far out of my normal universe that I had to find a way to protect myself, I guess.

"Plus, you made this huge point about not wanting a family and I thought, why tell him? Why bring him into this at all? And I was wrong. I should have told you."

"Yeah," he said tightly. "You should have. But some things are hard to talk about. To remember."

Was he talking about her now, or did he have secrets of his own? Was he going to tell her? Would he hold that part of himself back in some kind of retaliation for what Kate had done?

"Do you still love him?"

Her gaze snapped to his. "What?"

"Sam," Sean said, his gaze burning into hers. "Do you still love him?"

"I'll always love him, Sean," she said, knowing Sam deserved that much at least. "He was my husband, and he died. That's not something I can just tuck away and forget."

Kate had loved Sam with all the sweet promise of first love, and she would always treasure those memories. But what she felt for Sean was so much bigger, deeper, richer, there was simply no comparison. Sam had been as soft and gentle as a candle's glow. Sean was the sun—searingly bright, all-encompassing and so hot you risked being incinerated by getting too close.

Yet she couldn't stay away.

He moved in on her, and Kate shivered. It wasn't the wind, not the sea-scented cold; it was the heat in Sean's eyes that affected her. God, she loved him, and she knew she shouldn't. Knew she should find a way to stop.

He set his hands at her waist and whispered into the wind, "Who are you thinking of when I kiss you, Kate? Sam? Or me?"

Is that what had been tearing at him for days? How could he imagine that there would be room for anyone else in her mind when he was touching her? Hadn't he felt her surrender?

Lifting one hand, she cupped his cheek and told him the truth. "Don't you know? Don't you feel it when you touch me? It's you, Sean. There's only you."

"Good answer," he murmured, then bent his head and kissed her.

Here was what she wanted, *needed*. Here, Kate thought, was everything she couldn't have. She sank into his kiss, letting the cold wind wrap itself around her as counterpoint to the heat pumping from Sean's body into hers.

His arms were like iron, his heart pounding hard against hers. The taste of him filled her, and she gave herself up to the wonder of what she had with him. Her mind raced ahead, shouting warnings that were coming too late to prevent the hurt she would feel when this time with him was over. Deliberately, she closed down her mind, shut her worries away for another time. Now was all that mattered.

All she really had.

Waking up with Kate sprawled across his chest didn't bring even the tiniest bubble of panic. Sean told himself he should probably worry about that. He never had women stay over. Hell, he didn't normally bring women to his place—he went to theirs. This condo had been a sanctuary for him. His place in the world that was inviolate. But for the last week, he'd had Kate there with him and it felt…way too good.

She stirred, woke up slowly, slid her foot along his leg and his body went from sated to hungry in a blink. Tipping her head back, she looked up at him and gave him a slow smile.

"Good morning."

He grinned at her. "Getting better every second."

Rolling her over onto her back, he looked down into her eyes and stroked his hands up and down her body, relearning every line, enjoying the new curves caused by the gentle swell of her belly. He kissed her there, above his child's heart, and then moved up, to take her mouth in a kiss that showed her just how badly he needed her. She dragged her hands through his hair and the slide of her fingers was the kind of torture, he thought, a man would be willing to die for.

Kate arched into him as he stroked her core, and she sighed his name as her hips rocked into his hand. When that first gentle release claimed her, Sean moved to cover her body with his. He felt the tremors still claiming her when he entered her on a whisper.

Dawn streaked the sky with shades of pink and violet and red as he rose over her and moved into her heat with a tenderness he'd never experienced before. She met him with the same gentle touches, the quiet sighs and the murmured words that made sense only when two people became one.

Sean stared into her eyes and watched as the climax took her. She cried out his name, and he buried his face in the curve of her neck when his body surrendered and emptied into hers. And locked together, they fell.

A couple of hours later, they were back at the office. While Sean made dozens of phone calls, checking in with distributors, shipping, retailers and wholesalers, he knew Kate was working with Jenny in the art department.

They'd settled into a routine over the last few days. Breakfast on the terrace—and how great was it that Kate not only knew how to cook, but also *enjoyed* it? His condo now always had some delicious scent wafting through it.

He liked their early-morning time together, laughing, talking, just the two of them. Sean had never enjoyed a woman as much. He loved the way her mind worked—she was smart, creative and the strongest woman he'd ever known. He admired that about her, too. She didn't want to be taken care of, or told what to do and had no problem standing up and telling him so.

Every other woman he'd ever been with had *wanted* him to be in charge. But Kate had built a life for herself on her own terms. She'd lost her husband and hadn't curled up into a ball to whine about it. She hadn't felt sorry for herself. On her own, she'd turned her construction company into a thriving business, and now she was determined to raise a child on her own. Not that he was going to stand still for that.

He frowned, kicked back at his desk and shifted his gaze to the backyard garden. Color flowed in a serpentine spill across the length of the yard. Silky vines with bright yellow flowers climbed a trellis, and the birdbath Jenny had brought home from her and Mike's honeymoon trip to Paris held center stage on the lawn.

Celtic Knot had seen a lot of changes over the last couple of years. Brady was married, living in Ireland and the father of a baby boy. Mike was married now, too, about to be the father of a baby boy and letting his wife drag him around on house-hunting missions.

"And me?" Sean mused aloud. "Having a daughter with my lover, who's already started talking about getting back to Wyoming."

He'd noticed she was getting antsy, and he knew she was ready to get home and back to work. What he didn't know was what the hell he was going to do when she left. How was he supposed to live in his condo when every corner of the place would now remind him of her? Hell, he wouldn't even be able to sit out on the terrace without thinking about homemade pancakes and syrup-flavored kisses.

No. Unacceptable. Sean made his living talking people into seeing things his way. He made deals, solved problems and always managed to come out on top. There's no way he'd lose now. Not when Kate was more important than any other challenge he'd ever faced.

He wanted Kate Wells. He wanted their child, and he wouldn't lose either of them.

In the art department, most of the artists were on computers, a few at long conference tables scattered with paper and pencils and markers in a vast rainbow of colors. Energy seemed to sizzle in the air. Kate enjoyed the atmosphere in here, with everyone working together on one project and yet separately, each doing their best to make the whole work.

It reminded her of job sites back home. Whatever project they had going at the time, each of her crew would do their best work on their own, making sure that the finished product was cohesive. She admired creativity, too, and spending the last week watching these people bring myths to life had been fascinating.

"I never realized how much work went into creating a video game," she said.

"Believe me," Jenny told her with a grin, "I know just what you mean. When I first started working here, I was overwhelmed by all of the minutiae that goes into the design and the artwork and the graphics. But now I love it." She eased back in her chair and laid one hand over her growing baby.

Kate did the same and thought how nice it was to be able to share with a friend exactly what she was feeling. Their due dates only a couple of weeks apart, the two women had done some serious bonding over the last week. "Yours is a boy, right?"

"Yep. Mike's so excited, it's adorable." Jenny smiled to herself. "Keeps bringing home footballs and baseball gloves. But you know what I'm talking about. Sean's thrilled about having a daughter. I heard him telling Mike that his girl would be the first female pitcher in the big leagues one day."

Kate rubbed her belly and smiled gently. Sean was excited. He wanted their baby as much as she did and though she was happy about that, it was also a worry. She couldn't see how they would work this out.

For the past week, it had felt as if the two of them were playing house. Sleeping wrapped in each other's arms, waking up together, sharing breakfast on the terrace, talking about their days over dinner. She'd gone to the beach to watch him surf and had felt like a teenaged girl when her boyfriend came running out of the surf to flop down onto the sand beside her.

They spent every night making love in the big

bed with a view of the ocean, and every morning she woke to his kisses.

How was she supposed to go home and pretend she didn't miss it? Didn't miss him?

But she had to go home. Soon. Her crew needed her, she had a house, a life to get back to and pretending this time with Sean was real wouldn't change any of that. She knew, though, that the minute she talked about leaving, that would spawn another argument.

"How do you do it?" Kate suddenly asked Jenny. "How do you handle being with a man who's so sure of himself all the time?"

Jenny laughed, searched through the stack of artist's renderings and said, "Oh, it's not easy sometimes, but it's never boring being with a Ryan." She found the picture she was looking for and reached out to grab a deep red marker. Quickly, expertly, she added a robe, lifted in an unseen wind, to the character on the page.

"That's really good," Kate said, turning her head so she could see the whole image.

"Thanks." Jenny shot her a quick grin. "Here's

one of our famous arguments. Mike insisted that the empress here should be short and twisted, your typical cartoon image of a bad witch. He wanted evil easily seen on her face." She snorted and shook her head, clearly amused. "I told him that evil is much scarier if it looks beautiful. We went around and around on it. It was a fun fight, but I eventually won."

"If it helps any," Kate told her, looking at the beautiful drawing, "I think you're right. She's gorgeous, but there's something dark in her eyes."

"Exactly!"

"Do you argue a lot? With Mike I mean," Kate asked, then added quickly, "I'm not being nosy, it's only that Sean and I seem to butt heads regularly. He's so damn stubborn."

Jenny laughed out loud this time and set the sketch aside once she was finished. "Our arguments are legendary. When we get going, everyone around here heads for cover. Mike's got a head like a rock and frankly, I'm just as hardheaded, so when we're on opposite sides, it can get loud.

"But oh, making up is so worth the battle," Jenny said on a dreamy sigh.

Funny, Kate thought now, she and Sam had never argued. They'd come from the same place, wanted the same things, it was just *easy* being with him. But if she was honest, at least with herself, Kate could admit that the fire between her and Sean was part of what made being with him so exciting.

"Kate," Jenny said, sympathy coloring her tone, "I know it's none of my business, but are you planning on staying with Sean?"

The simple question, quietly asked, suddenly clarified everything in Kate's mind. She couldn't stay. Her life was in Wyoming and Sean's was here. Staying with him, living with him, was only making the inevitable harder on both of them. She had to get back to her real life and the sooner the better, for both their sakes. Meeting Jenny's eyes, she said, "No. I'm going home. Tomorrow."

Now, she had to tell Sean.

That night, they had dinner at a local diner, went to a summer concert in the park and then took a long walk back to the condo. Sean had been making plans all day, and he knew he had everything worked out. There was really only one way to solve their situation, he assured himself. All he had to do was convince her he was right. And since he was right so often, how hard would that be?

Once inside, they took the elevator to the penthouse level and walked into his home. In the last week, he realized Kate had made some changes not only to him, but also to this place. There were fresh flowers in vases, fruit in a bowl on the counter and the scent of the chocolate chip cookies she'd made the night before still in the air. Kate's stamp was all over this once-empty space—and on him, as well.

"You want a cookie?" she asked, heading for the kitchen.

"No," he said and stopped her by snatching her hand and pulling her up tight to him. "I want to talk to you."

"Okay." She reached up and laid one hand on his heart. "I have to talk to you, too."

"Well, ordinarily I'd say ladies first, since my mother would kick me if I didn't." He grinned at her. "But I've been thinking about this all day, and I want to get it said."

She smiled at him, and her eyes sparkled. "Okay, what is it?"

"I've been giving this situation we're in a lot of thought," he said, his hands on her shoulders, his thumbs caressing her even as he held on to her. "And I think I've got the solution."

"Sean…"

"No," he said, shaking his head, "let me finish. Kate, we get along great. The sex is incredible, and we're having a baby together. I think you know there's only one real answer here. Marry me."

He'd surprised her. He could see that. But what he didn't see was excitement, pleasure. Instead, he read regret in her eyes, and a cold fist took hold of his heart and squeezed.

"No."

Sean didn't have a quick comeback. He'd expected an argument. Hell, he'd been looking forward to it. He liked fighting with her almost as much as taking her to bed. But the look on her face told him she wasn't interested in arguing. She'd already made her decision. It was just one he couldn't live with.

"No? That's it?"

"You don't really want to marry me, Sean."

"See," he said, "I think I do, since I'm the one who proposed."

"That wasn't even a question," she pointed out, shaking her head. "You said 'marry me.' Like, I don't know, 'fetch me my slippers' or something."

"I don't own slippers."

"Not the point." She held up both hands and breathed deeply before saying, "I've been married before, and I don't want to risk that kind of pain again."

"There doesn't have to be pain," he countered. "I'm not talking about love here. A marriage based on mutual need is safe. Neither of us risks more than we're prepared to lose. It's the perfect solution, Kate. You know it is."

He thought he had her for a second when she chewed her bottom lip and seemed to be considering it, but then she started talking again. "I don't need you to take care of me, Sean. And I can take care of myself, so why should I marry you?"

He went tight and still inside. She didn't need him. Just like Adrianna.

"Besides, my life is in Wyoming and yours is here. I can't give up the mountains in exchange for crowds and traffic—not even for you. And I know you don't want to leave the ocean, so it won't work. I appreciate the offer but—"

"Spare me the appreciation," he snapped. Damn it, he was talking about marrying her, and she couldn't have been less interested. First time ever that he proposes and he gets turned down? Was it some kind of karmic kick in the butt? Was the universe at large having a good laugh at his expense?

He'd been so sure this was the solution. All the time he'd spent thinking how much he admired her strength and self-confidence, and it turned out that's exactly what was keeping her from agreeing to marry him.

"And what do we do about the baby?" he demanded.

"I promise, I will give you regular updates on how she is," Kate told him, her gaze locked with his. "And I won't try to keep her from you, either."

"That's it?" He slid his hands up from her shoulders to cup her face. "Just 'no' and we're done?"

"We'll never be done," she said and lifted her hands to cover his. "We'll always share a daughter."

He was going to take another stab at it. Sean and his partners hadn't built Celtic Knot by giving up. He had to fight for what he wanted or it wasn't worth getting. "It's not enough, damn it. We're good together, and you know it, Kate."

"I do," she agreed and stepped back, distancing them just a little. "But you're dangerous to my heart, Sean, and I don't want to risk that again."

"Nobody said anything about *love*, Kate." He

cared for her, of course he did. And she was the mother of his daughter. But he didn't *love* her. Love hadn't been a part of this at all for him. Love was something that tied a man into knots and sent him spinning off on roads he'd never planned to travel. It was having to think of someone else before yourself. And for a selfish man, that was hard to imagine.

She took a breath, blew it out and said softly, "I'm saying it, Sean. I made the mistake of falling in love with you, and now I have to leave so I can get over it."

He felt the punch of her words, saw the look in her eye and just for a second the world seemed to tilt. "What?"

"I love you, Sean. Didn't mean to, didn't want to." She shrugged and gave him a reluctant smile. "Turns out you're just as charming as you said you were. You got to me when I thought no one else ever could. But I can't be in love, Sean. I won't let myself be. So I can't marry you."

She wouldn't marry him, but she *did* love him. What the hell? Sean took a long step back, physically and mentally. He thought of his brother and how Mike's life had changed the minute he'd admitted to loving Jenny. Sure, he seemed happy, but he didn't have a pool table in his family room anymore, did he? And Brady? Hell, Brady had given up his home and moved to Ireland of all places because he was in love.

Well, Sean's world was already just as he liked it. He did what he wanted when he wanted. If that made him a selfish bastard, he'd just have to live with it.

"So when are you going home?" he finally asked, shoving both hands into his pants pockets.

"Tomorrow. I'll find the best flight I can—"

"Don't be ridiculous, take the company jet."

"I can't—"

"Damn it, Kate!" He took a breath to cool off and wondered why he was so angry. Sean didn't want love in his life any more than Kate did, so why did it make him furious that she loved him and wanted to "get over it" like a bad case of the flu?

"Don't yell at me," she said in a dangerously soft voice.

"Then don't say stupid things." Outrage glittered in her eyes, so he spoke up fast. "Sorry, sorry. Take the company jet. I don't want to have to worry about you on some crowded plane with strangers sneezing in your face and making my daughter sick."

A muffled laugh slipped from her and was gone again in a heartbeat. "Okay, thanks."

He rubbed the back of his neck then shook his head. "Yeah. No problem. You'll call me when you get home."

"Is that an order?" she asked.

"Damn straight it is," he told her, then pulled her in for a hug. And as he held her, Sean realized he really didn't want to let her go.

# Ten

The next morning, Kate was gone. She left early, with a kiss and a promise to stay in touch. And Sean let her go.

What choice did he have? She was the one who'd brought love into this. He'd been after a simple arrangement between lovers. Between parents of a child they both wanted. What the hell did love have to do with this anyway?

Kate leaving was for the best, he told himself. It just didn't feel like it at the moment. But instead of thinking about her or having to spend too much time in a condo that seemed to echo with emptiness, he threw himself into the launch of the new game.

So far, "The Wild Hunt" looked to be their biggest success yet. Sean spent hours every day on the phone, tracking numbers, making new contacts and negotiating new deals with their old customers. The packagers were having a hard time keeping up with demand for the game, and that was good news.

When the first sales reports began trickling in, Sean and Mike made a video call to Ireland so all three partners could talk about the latest news.

"The European numbers are every bit as exciting," Brady told them with a wide grin. "We've got more orders than we can fill—I ordered a second run at the packagers so we can move quickly and take advantage of the buzz the game's getting."

"Good idea," Sean said.

"And," Brady added, "I'm thinking we should line up an extra packager before we launch 'Dragon's Tears' this Christmas. We don't want to be caught coming up short again."

"Makes sense," Sean agreed, looking to Mike and getting a nod in response. "I've been scouting for more packagers already, since we've had the same problem here, needing an extra run to fulfill orders. Think I've lined up a new one— in Montana of all places, so I thought I'd go and check it out this week. Get things rolling way ahead of schedule."

"Montana. Isn't that close to Wyoming?" Brady swiveled in his desk chair and behind him, they caught glimpses of the Irish countryside, complete with dark gray skies and trees twisting in the wind.

"It is," Mike told him from his chair behind the desk. "And no, he's not stopping off to see Kate."

"Why the hell not?" Brady asked. "She's having your baby, you idiot."

"Thanks for all the support, guys," Sean said tightly, aiming a narrow-eyed stare at his friend and then at his brother. "But I think I can handle my own life, thanks."

"Not from where I'm sitting," Mike muttered.

"Me, either," Brady chimed in. He scowled into

the camera. "Did you learn nothing from watching Mike and I make messes of everything?"

"Yeah, I learned that being in love is mostly a pain in the ass," Sean said and took a sip of his beer.

It was after hours in the office. Everyone else had left for the day. Soon Mike would be heading home to be with Jenny, and Sean would be... alone. And that was how he liked it, he reminded himself.

"Hey, loving Jenny's the best thing I ever did," Mike argued.

"Yeah?" Sean tipped his head to one side and gaped at his brother. "How many times have you complained about losing your damn pool table? Or how many houses has Jenny had you out to look at this week?"

Mike sighed. "Eight. And I'll get another pool table when she finally decides on a house."

Sean snorted. "And you." He looked at Brady. "You moved all the way to Ireland for your wife."

"Best move I ever made."

Sean wasn't convinced. He'd watched Mike and

Brady take the plunge and though he'd encouraged them both, he just couldn't see himself taking the same fall.

"Jenny told me she talked to Kate this morning," Mike said.

Sean whipped his head around to look at him. "Why? Is everything okay with her?"

"Did you see that?" Mike asked Brady, then snorted at Sean. "Yeah, you don't care about Kate. I can see that now."

"I never said I didn't *care*," he argued. "I said I didn't *love* her."

"Sell it to someone who might buy it," Brady said and even all the way from Ireland, the sarcasm in his tone rang loud and clear.

Sean took a breath and told himself not to let them get to him. "Fine. Just tell me what she wanted when she called Jenny."

"I don't know." Mike shrugged. "Something about the baby moving around a lot and Kate wondering if Jenny's baby was doing the same thing."

Moving around a lot. And he wasn't there to

experience it with her. That chewed at him. Hell, it had been her choice to leave. He'd wanted her to stay, hadn't he? Asked her to *marry* him, for God's sake, when he'd never wanted to marry anyone. She'd been gone four weeks now, and missing her was just part of his life. He still couldn't walk into his own damn house without seeing her, smelling her, wanting her.

He gritted his teeth and said, "I'll call her tomorrow and check in."

"Yeah," Mike said, nodding with a smirk on his face. "Give the mother of your kid a phone call. Good idea."

"What're you riding me for?" Sean turned in his chair to glare at his brother.

"Because you're being a damn fool and it irritates me."

"Me, too," Brady said from Ireland.

"Thanks." Sean gave his friend a hard look. "Nothing like being insulted long-distance."

"What else do you want?" Mike leaned forward and slapped one hand down on his desk. "She's been gone a month, and you're more miserable to be around than ever."

Sean took a breath and huffed it out in a long sigh. Maybe he had a point. But hell, it wasn't like Mike was a vacation to hang out with half the time.

"Look," Sean said, trying for reasoned calm, "Kate had to go back home. She has work. I have work here. It's no big deal."

Could they hear the lie? he wondered. Could they see that his tongue nearly rotted and fell off just telling that lie? She said she didn't need him. And the bottom line was what had punched at him the hardest. Adrianna had said the same damn thing, and he'd lived through it.

He'd be fine this time, too. If she didn't want him there, he'd stay the hell away. But he wouldn't walk out on his kid. That baby was *his,* and nothing would keep him from her. Not even her mother.

"So you're gonna let her make the call on this." Mike shook his head sadly, disappointment gleaming in his eyes.

Sean ignored it and gave his brother and friend each a hard stare. "My business. My life. Back off."

"Fine." Mike turned to face Brady and shrugged. "There's no cure for 'idiot.'"

"So I hear." Brady cleared his throat, checked a readout on his tablet and changed the subject. "We're already getting preorders for the Christmas game. With that video of 'Dragon's Tears' we tacked on to the end of 'The Wild Hunt,' gamers are primed. Hell, they haven't even finished this game and they're already talking about the next one."

"All good," Mike said shortly. "Sean, what's the story on this new distributor?"

He pulled out his notes and lost himself in the details he was most comfortable with. Going over plans and strategies, he focused on the work, because thinking about Kate would push him over the edge.

Kate had been back in Wyoming for two months, and she still woke up stretching her arm out across the mattress reaching for Sean. Starting every day with disappointment and misery was taking a toll. She was tired a lot of the time, and the growing baby was like a ticking personal clock. Every day brought her closer to delivery, to meeting her child for the first time. And every day reminded her that Sean wouldn't be with her.

He should have been there, experiencing it all with her. Every time the baby kicked, she thought, *Sean should feel this*. When she bought a crib and put it together herself, she thought how much more fun it would have been to have Sean helping. Even though his skill with tools was less than brilliant, they'd have been together, doing something for their daughter.

And the misery filled her.

Phone calls and video chats weren't enough. Seeing him, hearing him, only made her miss him more when the call was over. Molly did her best to distract Kate, Harry worried and hovered and her crew had all taken on more work to pick up the slack, since she wasn't at her most productive at the moment.

The familiar symphony of power tools and voices shouting to be heard welcomed Kate when she stepped into the hotel. Nearly finished now, the guys were just taking care of a few finishing touches. Today, detailed wood carvings were being added around the mantels of the fireplaces, and low cabinets were being added to the walls in the main dining room. They still had to replace some shingles on the roof and add a few hand-crafted flower boxes to the front porch railings, but then the work would be done, except for whatever the Celtic Knot artists would do to the interior walls. Most of the crew was now working on the individual cabins, and just looking at them as she walked out to the wraparound porch made Kate smile.

They looked as if they belonged in a Faery forest, with their curved roofs, arched doors and round windows. Details were coming to life, making each cabin different. Paint colors were bright and Kate thought her favorite had to be the sapphire-blue cabin with the emerald-green door. Gingerbread trim scrolled along the rooflines of each cabin and outlined every window. Every cabin even boasted a tiny gas fireplace and whimsical chimney crafted out of either copper or brick. It was a magical spot and she wished, damn it, that Sean was there to see it all.

When her phone signaled a video chat, her heart gave a quick jump and even the baby kicked as if she knew it was her daddy calling. Had he felt Kate thinking about him?

"Sean. Hi." He looked so good, she thought sadly. And so far away.

"How's it going, Kate?"

He was in his office, she thought, recognizing the space behind him. It was harder, somehow, now that she'd been with him in California. She could picture him in the office where they'd shared a pizza one night. Where he'd held her on his lap while he answered phone calls. Kate's heart twisted in her chest, and she sighed a little at the memories.

"Everything's good," she said, forcing a smile

she knew wouldn't so much as touch her eyes. "We've nearly finished the main hotel. Just some minor things left to do there. The crew's focused mainly on the cabins, and they're looking wonderful."

"Yeah?" A half smile curved his mouth briefly. She wanted to kiss it.

"See for yourself." She turned the phone around and moved it slowly, so the camera would catch at least four of the cabins, sitting like tiny jewels among the trees.

When she was looking at him again, he said, "They look excellent, Kate. Really." He rubbed the back of his neck, and she almost smiled at the gesture. She recognized it as what he did when he was stressed. Good to know that seeing each other like this was no easier on him than it was on her.

"I wanted to let you know we'll be sending a couple of our artists out to do the work on the walls," he said.

"Great." A spurt of hope shot through her as she asked, "Are you coming, too?"

"No," he said and deflated that bubble of expectation. "I've got meetings set up for the next two weeks that can't be put off."

"Right. Okay." She nodded and smiled again, not wanting to let him know how disappointed she was. It had been two months since they were together, and it felt like two years. "When will they be here?"

"Sometime next week. They'll move into a couple of the bedrooms there so they can be on-site, get the job done as quickly as possible."

"Then I'll bring some supplies in for them."

"That'd be great, thanks," Sean said, then his voice lowered to an intimate tone. "How are you doing, Kate?"

"I'm fine," she said, lifting her chin and refusing to give in to the aching loneliness beginning to throb inside her. "Went to the doctor yesterday. He says the baby's perfectly healthy and growing just as she should."

"Good," he said, his gaze locked with hers. "That's good. Um, Jenny says her baby's moving all the time now. Is ours?"

A sting of tears burned her eyes, but she blinked them back. He should *know*, she told herself. He should be there, feeling every kick and bump their child made. Maybe she should have accepted that marriage demand disguised as a proposal. But even as she thought it, Kate knew she'd done the right thing. If for no other reason than the fact that she loved him and he didn't feel the same.

"Yes," she said, shutting down those thoughts. "She was doing jumping jacks all last night. I hardly slept."

He frowned. "That can't be good. You need rest, Kate. You—"

"I'm taking care of myself, Sean," she interrupted him quickly. "Everything's fine. We're fine." She watched him nod, then she asked, "How about there? The game still selling well?"

"Best one yet," he said, but there was no excitement in his eyes.

"Good. That's good, too." God, they sounded so stiff with each other. Both of them talking and neither of them saying anything that mattered. Anything *real*.

"Kate!"

She looked up to see one of her workers shouting to her from one of the cabins. Kate held up one finger to let her know she was coming.

"Sean, I'm sorry. Lilah's got some issue in a cabin. I've gotta go."

"Right," he said. "Me, too. Look, I'll call you in a day or two, okay? And be careful, will you?"

"Don't worry. Take care of yourself, Sean," she said and gave in to the urge to touch the screen as if she could stroke her finger along his cheek.

Then he was gone and she went back to work.

Two weeks later, Sean was at his desk when Mike stuck his head in the office and shouted, "Jenny's in the hospital!"

Panic shone in his brother's eyes, so Sean leaped up, said, "I'll drive," and raced Mike to the car. It was a wild ride through beach traffic, and Sean pulled out all the stops. He weaved in and out of the cars on Pacific Coast Highway like a driver at the Indy 500. "What happened?"

Mike looked at him, eyes stricken. "Jenny was out shopping, started feeling bad. She says she started bleeding. The doctor told her to get to the hospital." He dragged in a deep breath and blew it out again. "God, Sean, how the hell would I live without Jenny? The baby?"

"You're not going to have to find out." Sean prayed he was right.

Mike's closed fist hammered down on his own thigh helplessly, relentlessly. "I should have gone shopping with her this morning. I was busy and so damn sick and tired of looking for the perfect couch, I backed off. Let her go off alone. Idiot. What was I thinking?"

"You were thinking she'd be perfectly fine shopping on her own. This is not your fault, Mike."

"Doesn't matter whose fault it is."

Sean was panicked now, too. A cold ball of dread sat in the center of his chest, but he held it back and talked his brother off the ledge. "You couldn't have known, Mike. For God's sake, she went to the doctor just yesterday and everything was fine."

"Well, it's not *now*," Mike snapped. "Can't you go any faster?"

"If we had wings!" But Sean stomped on the gas pedal and gave it everything the car had. While he drove like a crazy man, Mike called their parents and Jenny's uncle Hank and his new wife, Betty. Family needed family when things went to hell.

Sean zipped through yellow lights, and when he turned into the hospital parking lot at last, the tires screamed for mercy. He'd barely stopped before Mike was out and running to the emergency room. A few minutes later, car parked, Sean was in there, too, looking for his brother and praying everything was all right.

It should be all right. The day before, the doctor had given Jenny a clean bill of health. What the hell could have happened so quickly?

He saw Mike at reception, then his brother was hustled into the back and Sean was left to pace through a crowded waiting room with a TV tuned to a game show with an annoying host.

Sean hated hospitals. The smell of them. The hopelessness of them. Look into any one of the faces gathered here and you'd see desperation, fear and the wish to be absolutely *anywhere* but there. Minutes ticked into hours and still Sean knew nothing. Mike came out occasionally just to tell him they were waiting for the doctor and to keep Sean from going nuts with the lack of information.

Jack and Peggy Ryan hurried into the waiting room and after hugs and whispered conversations, they sat down on the most uncomfortable chairs in the world to wait.

Sean couldn't sit. Couldn't stand still, either. He kept pacing. He walked through the room until his mother told him to go outside because he was giving her a headache. So he went and tipped his face into the ocean breeze. But there was no peace there, either, since Jenny's aunt and uncle raced up a few minutes later demanding answers.

And the whole time he waited and worried for

his brother and sister-in-law, his mind kept turning to Kate. What if this had happened to her? Hell, for all he knew, it could be happening right now. He was hundreds of miles away. If she had a crisis, chances were good he wouldn't find out about it until it was over. What if she was out on a damn job site and something happened and she was alone?

Panic was alive and clawing at him as he wondered if Kate was telling him everything. What if she wasn't really okay? Or if there was a problem with the baby? How the hell would he know? He stomped back inside and saw his mother and Betty holding hands and whispering while Hank and Jack sat stone-faced.

Through the raging storm in his mind, Sean realized something that seemed profound yet it shouldn't have been. *This* was love. Families coming together in a crisis. Leaning on each other. Being there. His heart opened and heat spilled out, filling every vein in his body.

He looked at his parents, who'd come through problems of their own and emerged stronger than ever. And there was Betty, who'd been Hank's housekeeper for years until finally one day they both woke up and realized that what kept them together was *love*. Yeah, Brady had moved to Ireland, but he loved it. And Mike lost his beloved pool table, but what had he gotten instead? A woman to share his life with.

Love didn't stifle anything. It blossomed and grew and made lives richer. And Sean was certifiable for trying to avoid the knowledge that he *loved* Kate. Maybe he had from the beginning—he didn't know. What he was sure of was that night at the view point. Something major had shifted inside him and he'd loved her then and loved her now.

Someone in the waiting room sobbed, and the sound raked along his spine like nails on a chalkboard. *Kate*. Her name echoed over and over in his mind. A chant. A prayer. The last two months without her had been the longest, loneliest of his life. He'd let her go because she said she loved him but didn't need him.

"That's a damn lie," he muttered, flicking a

glance toward the closed doors separating him from his family. "Of course she needs me. As much as I need her. And I'm going to tell her so the minute—"

Mike rushed through the double doors and hurried to the family. He was surrounded instantly with everyone asking questions at once. Until Hank clapped his hands and said, "One at a time."

"She's okay, so's the baby," Mike said first and on cue, Peggy and Betty wept. "Doc says she's been doing too much and lifting too much, which is what I've been telling her, but who listens to me?"

He was smiling as he complained, and Sean could see the stark relief on his face. "I'm taking her home in a couple hours, so you guys can come see her then if you want."

"We will," Betty told him and rose up to kiss his cheek. "You give her our love and tell her I'll be there tomorrow to look after her."

"I will, thanks."

Peggy kissed her son and said, "I'll be there with Betty, and we'll make sure she stays put."

"Thanks, Mom."

When the family left, Mike turned to Sean and breathed a huge sigh.

Everything was forgotten except for Jenny and her baby. "She's really okay?"

"Yeah," Mike said, smiling. "Scared me brainless, but she's okay. Come say *hi* to her." Sean kept pace with his big brother through the double doors and down the hall until they came to a curtained-off bed in the corner. Mike pushed the drapes wide and there was Jenny, propped up on pillows and smiling. "Hi, Sean, I'm so sorry I scared you guys."

"Hey, don't worry about us." At the side of her bed, Sean lifted her hand and gave it a squeeze. "You okay?"

"I'm fine. The baby's fine, too." She rubbed her belly, then stretched out her hand for Mike, linking the three of them. "His heartbeat is strong, and he's kicking up a storm. All good."

Mike lifted her hand and kissed it, and Sean's heart ached for the fear his brother had just lived through. "So what happened?"

"Apparently, I've been on my feet too much lately and—"

"Didn't I tell you that?" Mike interrupted, kissing her hand again as if making sure she was still there and safe.

"Yeah, yeah, you were right. God, I hate admitting that," Jenny said with a laugh. "Anyway, I get to go home, I just have to put my feet up more. Take it easy and quit spending all day exploring antique stores."

"Hallelujah," Mike muttered.

"That's great, Jenny, really." Sean bent over and kissed her forehead. "You take it easy and quit scaring everybody, okay? I want to talk to Mike a second, then I'll toss him back to you."

"Take your time," she said, smiling as she waved them both off. "He'll only hit me with 'I told you so' again anyway…"

Relief was almost painful, Sean thought. When every nerve in your body was filled with tension that was suddenly released, you were left a little shaky. He walked outside, with Mike right behind him.

"Man, I've never been so scared in my life," Mike muttered, leaning back against the hospital's brick facade. "If this is what having kids is like, I'm gonna be an old man before I'm forty."

Sean slapped his brother's shoulder in solidarity. "I'm glad everything's okay, Mike."

"Yeah, me, too." He smiled, scrubbed both hands over his face. "Thanks, man. You were a rock. You came through for me."

"Always. You need me to take you guys back home?"

"No. Jenny's car's here. We're good."

"Okay." Nodding, Sean said, "Then I'm going to the condo to pack."

Mike's eyebrows lifted. "Going on a trip?"

"No," Sean told him. "I'm going home. To Wyoming."

The end of summer in Wyoming carried a hint of the fall to come in the breeze that danced in the trees and the thick, heavy clouds gathering on top of the mountains. Kate was really tired of being hot, so she was looking forward to fall and winter. Now, though, she ignored the late summer sun and picked her way carefully across the forest floor.

Seth and Billie, the Celtic Knot artists, had finished up their work on the cabins and were now busily handcrafting the murals in the main hotel. With her crew busy on a job site in town, Kate wanted to take a look at the gazebo they'd erected last week. No ordinary lakeside pavilion, this structure was as fanciful as the jewel-toned cabins nestled in the pines.

Scrollwork highlighted every pillar, and the bench seats followed the hexagonal line. There were carved dragons perched on the roofline like gargoyles and the view of the lake was just as mystical. Sean really was going to have an amazing place when it was all finished. Kate walked up the gazebo steps and sat down, because at seven months pregnant now, she was just tired.

But more than tired, she felt…sad. She lifted her face into the wind and thought of last winter and those precious snowbound days with Sean.

She wished he was there with every beat of her heart.

"You know," a voice said from right behind her, "I just realized how much I missed this place."

Kate gasped and spun around to look at Sean walking toward her in long, purposeful strides. He wore a black T-shirt, black jeans and boots. His black hair blew in the wind, and his sharp blue eyes were locked on her with so much heat she could barely breathe. If this was a dream, she didn't want to wake up.

He came up the steps of the gazebo, then paused to turn and look around. "The trees, the mountains, the sky—" He shot her a look and a half smile. "God, you're beautiful. I really missed looking up and seeing all those stars every night, too."

"I can't believe you're here." Kate stood up slowly, her gaze locking with his.

"Believe it." His gaze was steady, his voice warm and strong. "I'm here because I missed *you*, Kate. Like I'd miss my right arm, I miss you."

"God, Sean—"

He shook his head and moved up to her in one long stride. Then he put one finger against her mouth to keep her quiet. "Nope. I came a long way to have my say, and I just want you to listen."

As glad as she was to see him, Kate wasn't going to stand there and be shushed. From behind his finger, she grumbled, "Excuse me?"

"There's my girl." He laughed and shook his head again. "Damn if I haven't missed that stubborn streak of yours." Before she could argue that ridiculous point, he bent and kissed her fast and hard, then lifted his head to look at her again.

Her lips were buzzing, her heart pounding. Even the baby felt like she was jumping up and down inside, as if she sensed her mother's excitement.

"We're getting married, Kate—"

She inhaled, but he cut her off.

"Before you start in on not wanting to risk more pain, think about the pain we've both been in for the last two and a half months," he stressed. "Admit it, Kate. You can't lie to yourself or to me about this. We've been too separate, lonely, miserable."

"We have, but…married?" She'd already done that, and it had ended in heartbreak. And if she lost Sean as she'd lost Sam…she didn't think she'd survive it.

Sean laughed and sighed all at once. "I can see in your eyes exactly what you're thinking, Kate. But see, the thing is, I love you."

She swayed a little and was grateful he took hold of her.

"Yeah. Surprised the hell out of me, too," he admitted. "But more than that, I *need* you. And you need me."

Kate wanted to argue that, but what would be the point? They would both know she was lying. Of course she needed him. And missed him. And loved him.

"See," he said softly, "when you said you didn't need me, that kind of gave me a hard punch." He blew out a breath and scowled. "We all have secrets, Kate. It wasn't only you in that boat. Ten years ago, I thought I was in love and she got pregnant and I…let her down." His features softened in memory then hardened in shame. "I wasn't what she needed because I was too selfish to see past my own life."

"Sean, I'm sorry…"

"She lost the baby, Kate, and then told me to leave because she didn't need me around anymore." He shrugged. "So, when you said it, I just pulled back and locked down. Stupid."

"Not stupid," she said, her heart breaking for him. They all had losses, she thought now. Everyone had pain; no one got through life with just a series of one rainbow after another. "I lied, you know. I do need you."

"Yeah," he said, with that half smile of smug satisfaction that she'd missed so much. "I know. So back to my first statement…we're getting married, Kate. And we're going to live here."

"In Wyoming?"

"Not just Wyoming, but *here*," he said. Keeping one arm around her shoulders, he turned her to point out to the strip of land that ran along the lake and backed up to the forest. "I'm hiring Wells Construction to build us a house, right there."

"A house," she whispered, looking from his face to the beautiful stretch of land.

"Our house. You're going to design it any way you want, Kate." He looked down into her eyes, and everything in her lit up like Christmas. "Make it your dream house, Kate, because all of our dreams are going to come true in it."

"But, Sean, what about the ocean?" she asked, stunned. "You love it so much. How can you give it up? And you'd be so far from your family…"

"You and the baby," he insisted, his eyes boring into hers, "are my family." His thumb stroked away a single tear that tracked from the corner of her eye, and his touch sent ripples of warmth sliding through her. Then he smiled again. "And with the company jet, we can travel as much as we want. We'll keep the condo, stay there when we visit. But meanwhile, I'll have the lake, and paddleboarding might be fun. You could even teach me to ski in the winter."

She laughed shortly. "You're crazy."

"Crazy about you."

God, Kate wanted to believe, to have everything he was offering her. To love and be loved. To make a family with him, to build a dream house on the shore of the lake and to make a lifetime of memories with this man who touched her so deeply.

"I'm just so scared of losing again." She reached up and cupped his face in her palms. "Sean, if something happened to you, I think it would kill me."

"I can't promise that nothing will ever go wrong, Kate. Nobody can." He led her to the bench seat, sat down and pulled her onto his lap. Kate stared into his eyes and heard every word when he spoke again. "If something goes wrong, we'll handle it. Together. But Kate, what if everything goes right? What if our lives are perfect and happy and filled with a dozen kids screaming and running through the forest?"

She laughed at that even as he laid the flat of his hand on the swell of their child. "A dozen?"

He shrugged. "Negotiable. But with all this room around here, I'd say we'll need at least six."

Kate could see it all. The two of them, a houseful of kids, taking part in the conventions he would hold on the grounds every summer. Working the hotel, being with Sean every day and night and she suddenly wanted it all more than her next breath.

"What's not negotiable," he was saying, "is marriage. I want you, Kate. Forever. So say yes."

"Yes," she said and felt a huge, smothering weight slide off her shoulders. This was right. They were perfect for each other, and together they would be able to handle anything that came at them.

"Hey!" Sean's gaze shot to her belly. "What was that?"

Kate laughed, delighted in the man. Throwing her arms around his neck, she said, "That was your daughter telling you she's glad her mommy and daddy are getting married."

"That's amazing," he said, wide-eyed as he laid his hand across her belly, waiting to feel it again.

"So, where's my engagement ring?" Kate asked, feeling loved and wanted and needed.

"Ha!" He reached into his pocket and pulled out a box. "No engagement ring, you'd only get it caught on a saw or some damn thing." Opening it, he showed her a pair of stunning emerald earrings. "This is for the engagement and plain gold bands for both of us when we get married."

"Oh, Sean…" Kate smiled through her tears. How perfect was it to be loved by a man who knew her so well? So intimately? "You really are perfect, aren't you?"

"Don't forget charming," he quipped, and then he kissed her.

# Epilogue

*Two months later*

"Kate, come on," Sean shouted, "the storm's rolling in, and I want to be off this mountain before we get snowed in again!"

He glanced around the main room in the hotel and waited impatiently for his wife. The whole place was furnished now—beds, couches, chairs and top-of-the-line entertainment systems with gaming capabilities in every room. They were ready for guests, but with the new baby coming, he'd made an executive decision to wait until spring for the grand opening. Give them a chance to settle into being a family first.

It was only early October, but winter was heading their way in a hurry. He never should have agreed to bring her up here today, but Kate was like a dog with a bone when she wanted something.

She'd been determined to get another look at the house site before the snow hit. She was working on the design so the architect could have the plans in time for the crew to get started on it as soon as winter was over. The woman was like a force of nature. She wanted everything done right and in her time.

"Kate! If you're not out here in ten seconds, I'm going back to your place without you!" An empty threat, and they both knew it.

"You know," Kate said as she came toward him, "if you were walking around with a bowling ball on your bladder, you'd move a little slowly, too."

Nine months pregnant and she still took his breath away. How could he love her more every day? She was frustrating and intriguing and everything he'd ever wanted in his whole damn life.

"Yes, you're right," Sean said, hustling her into her coat and easing her toward the door. "Men are miserable human beings and women should rule the world. Just get in the car, okay?"

"Relax, Sean," she said, stopping on the front porch to look around. "We're not going to be stuck, and I'm not having the baby here."

"Damn right you're not," he said, closing the door behind them and locking it up. Once the baby was born, he and Kate were thinking of moving up here and waiting out the winter. Kate's little bungalow was too small for the three of them, plus all of the office equipment Sean needed to get his work done for the company.

He was looking forward to the quiet. The solitude. And even being snowed in with Kate again—*after* the baby was born.

"It's nice that Jenny and Mike had their little boy yesterday," Kate was saying dreamily as he helped her down the front steps. "Now our Kiley and their Carter will only be a day apart in age."

"Yeah," he muttered, keeping her moving toward the car, "it's great. Wait." He stopped dead when what she'd said sunk in. "How do you know Kiley's coming today?" Suspicion then panic settled over him like a radioactive cloak. "Are you in labor?"

She grinned at him, went up on her toes and kissed him. "For the last hour or two. You're going to be a daddy today, Sean! Isn't that amazing?"

Joy, wonder, then one more time, *panic*. "We've got to get you to the hospital. Walk slow. No bumps. Don't breathe too hard."

She laughed and when he got her tucked into the car and raced around to the driver's side, he heard another peal of laughter and told himself women really were the stronger sex. Why wasn't she terrified?

Sean threw the car into gear and headed down the mountain as quickly as he could. Storm clouds gathered and began to surge forward, like an army on the march. He couldn't worry about them, though, because in the passenger seat, Kate groaned.

"Are you okay?"

"Fine," she muttered and shifted uncomfortably on the seat. "That one was much stronger, though. Just hurry, Sean."

When she started the panting and breathing, Sean's heart leaped into a wild gallop so frantic he almost forgot to breathe himself. The mountain road had never seemed so long or so twisty. He had to take his time or they'd go flying off the edge, but he had to hurry because he was *not* going to deliver his first child in his car.

Twenty minutes later, he pulled into the hospital lot and parked the car, not caring if it was legal or not. Kate was wincing and moaning regularly now. When he helped her out of the car, she grabbed hold of his hand and twisted with the strength of someone twice her size.

Sean gritted his teeth and went with it, steering her inside and standing by helplessly as orderlies appeared and whisked her into a wheelchair. She looked back at him as she disappeared down a long hallway, and Sean felt that thread of panic again when he lost sight of her.

But a few minutes later, he was in the labor room with her, and she battled and raged to bring their baby girl into the world. Sean's heart twisted every time a pain claimed her, and he would have given every dollar he had to change places with her. Anything would have been better than watching the woman he loved suffer.

"Don't look so worried, honey," she said, voice broken in between gasps. "This is normal. Everything's just moving really fast."

"This is fast?" He felt like they'd been doing this for days. "I was wrong before. Not six kids. One's enough. God, I swear I'll never touch you again, Kate."

She laughed, delighted, then gasped as another pain slammed home. "I'm not going to hold you to that, sweetie. Oh, Sean, she's coming."

Doctor Eve Conlon bustled in, and to Sean the woman looked like she was fourteen years old. Lots of curly, thick hair, big brown eyes and a wide smile. "How're we doing?"

"Kate says the baby's coming," Sean blurted. "How're you?"

Eve laughed. "Take a breath, Sean. I'm just going to take a look, Kate."

When the brief examination was over, the doctor smiled and announced, "Kate's right. She's doing everything in a hurry. Your daughter's on her way."

The next half hour was nothing but a blur for Sean. He'd never been so scared and elated all at the same time. Admiration and love for his wife soared as he watched her bring their baby into the world with a fierce determination that staggered him.

All he could do was hold her hand and look on in proud amazement when the doctor laid their gorgeous, screaming daughter on Kate's chest. Kate laughed and cried and smoothed her hands over their baby's tiny body, and Kiley, as if sensing she was just where she was supposed to be, settled right down and looked directly into her father's eyes.

Reverently, he reached out to touch her tiny hand, and the baby's fingers curled around one of his fingers in an instinctive grasp that took a firm hold on his heart, as well. "Happy birthday, Kiley Ryan," he whispered.

Love rose up and spilled over inside him, and Sean was humbled by it all. She was less than a minute old and already, Sean loved her more than he would have believed possible. He'd never known he could feel so much, so quickly. He looked at his beautiful wife and realized he had never guessed what it would mean to love a woman so completely.

"Thank you," he whispered and bent to kiss Kate. "Thank you for her and for everything you've given me since the day I met you."

"I love you, Sean," Kate said.

"Don't ever stop." Sean laid his hand over Kate's and together, they cradled their daughter—their future.

\* \* \* \* \*